TAKING COVER WITH THE RANCHER

BARB HAN

TORJAKE PUBLISHING

To my family for unwavering love and support. I love each and every one of you to the moon and back.

1

Crater Rock had always been Hudson Firebrand's salvation. This was the place he'd come when those early hormones tripped him up, pimples flared, and life stopped making sense. Thankfully, those awkward teenage years were long gone but now he was staring down a different milestone. His thirtieth birthday. Questions he'd never pondered before suddenly looped in his thoughts. Was he chasing his own dreams? Or was he doing what was expected of him instead of making his own way? Was he happy on the ranch? Or was the work so ingrained in him that he didn't know where it ended and he began?

To make matters worse, all eight of his brothers were engaged or married. Hudson brought his hand up to loosen his collar. He could barely commit to starting a taco business; there was no way he was ready for a lifetime commitment.

He scanned the landscape. There was barely a breeze and no relief in sight from the two-year drought scorching the land. Rivers were drying up. Forget the creeks. The lack of water was impacting Firebrand land, and nearby smaller ranches were doing a whole lot worse.

But today Hudson wasn't here for the view. His cousin Vaughn had requested a meeting. Vaughn and Hudson were the same age and had been close growing up until Vaughn ditched ranch life in favor of joining the military. He'd said something about needing to know if he could handle being an adult on his own terms. Growing up as a Firebrand, they'd had everything they could have asked for. There'd been plenty of food on the table, more than enough play-mates with eighteen cousins between the two brothers' families, and enough freedom to roam the land. They'd also learned how to put in a real day's work, care for things smaller and weaker than them, and do their part around the house. With nine hungry mouths to feed and no hired help, Hudson's mother had taught her sons early on how to set a table, clear a table, and pick up after themselves.

The Marshall's death had caused a rift in the family that seemed impossible to repair. They'd been at odds ever since their grandfather's unexpected passing early in the summer. Hudson's father and uncle had been fighting since long before, but it had gotten so much worse now. The cousins rarely spoke to each other any longer. It was as though the family had been split right down the middle, and there was no end in sight to the bickering about the Marshall's will. Since Vaughn had been away from Lone Star Pass since high school graduation, maybe he could offer a fresh perspective on how the ranch should have been split. His level head was never more needed than now.

Of course, the best course of action would be to get everyone in the same room and hash out their differences. Not let anyone leave until a fair settlement had been agreed upon by both sides. Their relationships might be impossible to salvage at this point. The thought of doing something to make matters worse was a sore spot. But then, it hardly seemed they could get worse. Something needed to give.

Was all the infighting responsible for Hudson's restlessness? Or was the taco business truly calling him away from everything he'd known? Taco business, he decided. Tacos were his future.

The first thing he needed to do when he was back in cell coverage range was put a message on the family group chat asking for a sit-down meeting. What happened with the land, cattle, and mineral rights was none of his business after he would let his father and brothers buy him out. He could wash his hands of the place and all the drama that had been plaguing the family for months, which should be freeing. So, why did his chest take a hit instead?

For one, Hudson had grown up here. He loved the land. He loved his family. He loved the business. Cattle ranching had been all he'd known before his interest in running a taco business. He wouldn't be human if the thought of leaving wasn't at least a small gut punch. Most of his hesitation about calling the meeting led back to his father's recent stroke. Hudson didn't want to create more stress. Since all eight of his brothers lived and worked here, his leaving would break up the family and their legacy.

Motion straight down and in his line of sight caught his attention. He saw someone systematically working their way toward him. Must be Vaughn. But since there'd been a significant amount of crime in Lone Star Pass recently, he took nothing for granted. Hudson squatted down and placed his hand on the butt of his gun just in case. People weren't the only threat on a ranch. Dangerous animals like hogs made roaming around without a means of protection impossible. Carrying had been a lifelong habit and he'd been taught how to handle a gun long before his tenth birthday. Being prepared had kept him alive. Poachers could be even more dangerous than nature out here.

Based on the size of the person coming toward Hudson, he reasoned it had to be Vaughn. And, hold on a second, there was someone else tucked right behind his cousin. The person was practically glued to Vaughn's backside. So much so, Hudson almost didn't see them. Vaughn hadn't mentioned anything about bringing someone with him.

Glimpses of the person revealed a small frame, a female figure. Was Vaughn married? Was he about to spring a wife on the family?

Another one bites the dust, Hudson thought as the famous Queen song thumped in the back of his mind. Vaughn's relationship status shouldn't send Hudson into another tailspin, but it was a shock. If Vaughn had mentioned her on the phone, then Hudson would be expecting her. Not to mention there'd been that unsettling something in Vaughn's voice during the call that had sent a cold chill racing down Hudson's spine; a cold chill that was back. There was also something about Vaughn's stance—protective?—and the way he kept checking from side to side that caused all the tiny little hairs on Hudson's neck to prick. His cousin kept stopping to survey the area and check behind them as though to make sure no one had followed. When he started walking again, he favored his left leg. The whole scenario was cause for unease.

There was no way to call Vaughn on his cell since this entire area was a dead zone. Hudson scanned the zone surrounding his cousin and the mystery woman. His gaze locked onto movement roughly thirty feet south from them.

Hudson drew his weapon and aimed toward the commotion. His finger hovered over the trigger mechanism of his Sig Sauer. From this distance, he couldn't get a good visual on whoever was following Vaughn.

Hunkering down, Hudson figured he could circle around and get close enough to see if he recognized the follower. If not, at least he could get off a shot to stop the jerk. Because those tiny hairs on the back of his neck were never wrong, and they sensed danger.

Navigating his way down in a zigzag pattern and quiet as a church mouse would give him an advantage. He already had the element of surprise. Considering he had no idea what his cousin had gotten himself into, Hudson would ask questions first and shoot as a last resort. Shooting was always a last resort.

Twenty feet down and he made eye contact with Vaughn. Of course, his cousin would have seen Hudson coming. Vaughn's military training would have kicked in, making it next to impossible to sneak up on him.

Hudson pointed toward his own eyes before pointing down the hill. The nod came quickly from Vaughn, who cut right instead of continuing the course toward the top. Hudson couldn't get a good look at the female figure tucked behind his cousin. All he could see so far was that she was considerably shorter than Vaughn. Considering the average height of a Firebrand came in around six-feet-four-inches, most people fell into her category.

A whole bunch of questions swirled about Vaughn and the mystery woman. None could be asked or answered at the moment, so Hudson kept zigzagging and making his way down toward the trespasser.

By the time Hudson made it where the guy should be, he was gone. The ground was hard and dry from lack of rain, making it impossible to locate footprints or any indication which direction the person went. Had they figured out

Hudson was tracking them? Had they realized Vaughn had changed course?

Hudson's immediate next thought was Honey. If anything happened to his mare, Hudson would lose it. He circled back to where he'd tied off the reins and his heart rammed the inside of his ribcage when he realized she was gone.

Even with the dry, cracked soil, Honey had enough weight on her to leave impressions. He followed them and listened for sounds of her hooves pounding the ground. Anyone with access to a horse would be keen on getting far away if the person had realized they'd been spotted. This person had to have figured out Hudson was on the hunt.

He bit back a curse as he dropped to the ground and put his ear against the dirt. He heard hooves there. Not running. Not thundering in the opposite direction. Slow, methodical walking.

Which meant, the rider was using the horse for a height advantage. Then, there was the obvious fact the person could get away much quicker on horseback than on foot.

Seriously, what had Vaughn brought back to the ranch with him?

A FEW MINUTES were all it had taken for Anisa Turner's life to go from nurse on her day off, to woman on the run. One minute she was taking her brother's ATV out for a spin on her day off and the next she'd come across a man who was bleeding and too weak to crawl out of the ravine he'd fallen into. At least, she'd believed he'd fallen inside. Later, she realized he'd climbed in on purpose before getting stuck.

It struck her as strange how normal life could be in one

minute and how upside down it could be in the next, changing at the speed of a finger snap. She still had no idea what was going on or how she'd ended up here on Firebrand property. All she knew for certain was that she was on a famous ranch with someone who had a very famous last name. This massive plot of land that went on as far as the eye could see belonged to one of the wealthiest cattle ranching families in Texas, the Firebrands. She didn't have to be from around these parts to be familiar with them. They were the stuff of legends.

She'd spent the past two days nursing Vaughn Firebrand as a threat seemed to always be one step behind. Vaughn had been shot. The bullet had taken off a chunk of his thigh. He'd let himself bleed too much before stopping to rest and address his wound. He'd said it had been a necessity. And then they'd spent the past twenty-four hours trying to get here, on foot. Speaking of which, hers were swollen, pulsing, and angry. In the beginning, she'd accompanied the injured man in order to keep him alive. That was before she'd been seen, when being on this little journey was voluntary. Now, whoever was after Vaughn was trying to get her too.

Anisa needed to stop. She squeezed Vaughn's hand, the signal she needed a break. If he could risk it, she would get minutes to regroup. If not, he did his best to find a hiding spot until the threat passed. Anisa hadn't said anything to him and had no plans to, but her baby hadn't moved since yesterday. At twenty-seven years old, Anisa was pregnant and alone.

A twig snapped to their right. Someone was close by.

Vaughn froze after tucking her behind him. He'd been very protective of her and the baby after he'd regained consciousness three days ago. He'd also told her to get far away from him the minute he saw her stomach. The warning, unfortunately, had come a little too late.

The air was so still, they were so quiet, Anisa could have sworn she heard her own heartbeat. She said a silent protection prayer the baby was all right as she rubbed her belly with her free hand.

"It's Hudson. Don't shoot," the unfamiliar man's voice wrapped around her. There was a comforting quality that made her believe she might get out of this situation in one piece, which was strange considering she hadn't even seen the person's face yet.

Vaughn headed toward the voice and before she realized, the two were in a bear hug. The man who stepped out of the trees with Vaughn was similar in height. He had to be at least six-feet-four-inches. His dark hair had sun-kissed highlights that came from working outdoors, a five o'clock shadow that looked more like a beard, and dark brown irises with the thickest, blackest set of lashes. And then a dimpled chin that softened an otherwise carved from granite jawline.

The inappropriate surge of attraction caught Anisa off guard. She shoved it aside as Vaughn made introductions.

"This is my cousin Hudson," Vaughn said to her. "You'll be able to trust him one hundred percent."

"Good to meet you. I'm Anisa," she said to the man whose eyes seemed locked onto her stomach. He immediately shifted his gaze up to hers. Questions danced in those serious brown eyes of his, but they would have to wait.

"It's a pleasure to meet you," he said with a quick smile and a nod before turning his attention back to Vaughn. "What's happening?"

"I never would have involved you if I'd known they would follow me here," Vaughn said to his cousin. The family resemblance was striking but there was something special about Hudson.

"Who are you talking about?" Hudson asked. "Who followed you?"

Anisa perked up because Vaughn hadn't exactly been chatty about the threat they'd been facing.

"There's no time to explain," Vaughn said in practically a whisper. It was the same thing he'd said to her several times since this three-day journey had begun. "We should split up. I can get their attention and drive them east. Why don't the two of you head northwest?"

Hudson's gaze dropped to his cousin's wedding finger, then hers. He issued a sharp sigh. "You want me to be responsible for your—"

Vaughn cut him off with a severe headshake.

"I'm responsible for her," he corrected. "This is my fault."

He'd said those exact four words to her more times than she could count in the past couple of days. Whoever was after him was now a threat to her as well. Anisa had moved to Texas to outrun her past and had been successful. What did it matter? It seemed tragedy and destruction would follow wherever she landed.

Apparently, she was now in someone's crosshairs because she'd stopped to help a human in need. She'd done so because she could. She'd had the ability to clean his wound, not to mention the supplies on hand. Those weren't something most people went camping with, he'd said. He'd quieted right down after she told him what she did for a living.

It made sense she would be prepared. Being a nurse was only half the reason. The half she was willing to share with a stranger. Her younger brother had been the other half. T.J.

was a year and a half younger than Anisa. Same father, different mothers. She'd moved to Austin to be closer to him. Then had to watch him spiral after he got addicted to pain medication following an ATV accident. He'd never recovered emotionally from losing one leg and having another that was 'for show' as he'd put it. He'd been paralyzed from the waist down in the crash, a crash that had taken everything from him.

Before he'd overdosed, he'd made her promise to go camping once a year on his birthday and take the ATV out in his honor. Anisa had agreed and then realized how crazy she was for consenting. She wasn't a camper let alone someone who went around on an ATV.

She issued a sharp sigh. T.J. had only been gone a year but it all seemed like yesterday. With his death, she'd lost the only family she had left. Three months later, she'd lost her best friend and the man she was supposed to marry. Bad luck followed her like a stalker in a dark alley.

And now, her child had stopped moving.

2

"I'll head northwest," Hudson said after a long pause. He'd noticed his cousin was nursing a limp. "Be careful."

"Always am," Vaughn said with a wink. "What kind of supplies did you bring?"

"Enough for lunch. But that's gone along with Honey. The bastard took my horse," Hudson ground out.

"We'll get her back," Vaughn stated with resolve. He shot Hudson a look that said he knew how much losing his horse must sting.

"I have no doubt about it," Hudson shot back. He wasn't leaving this area until he found his mare. Taking care of Vaughn's pregnant girlfriend or wife complicated matters, considering he needed to take her away from the danger and away from Vaughn.

"If we don't meet up again, promise me you'll make sure Anisa is safe," Vaughn said in a foreboding tone.

"Hold on a minute. What exactly is going on here?" Hudson asked, needing to know what kind of threat they faced.

"I'll explain later," Vaughn said, surveying the area. He started back up the hill before Hudson could argue.

Then again, he had Anisa. He could ask her as he moved her toward safety.

"Keep your phone on you," Vaughn stated. "I'll call as soon as I can and have service."

"Will do," Hudson said, sensing the urgency.

His cousin almost immediately disappeared into the trees. The sound of twigs snapping to their right caused Hudson to reach for Anisa's hand. A timid deer moved away from them as though heading toward the meadow.

"Are you okay?" he asked Anisa, unsure of what to do with a pregnant person. Could she run?

"I have to be," she responded with a quick glance down at her belly. The bump wasn't huge and he had no way of knowing how far along she was anyway. She couldn't be too far considering it didn't look like a basketball had been tucked underneath her shirt. In fact, from the back, he could scarcely tell there was a baby in there.

A baby? Vaughn a father?

Even Hudson's cousins were starting to drink the ranch water, he thought as he led Anisa away from the noise. She wasn't as quiet as he'd hoped. Any decent tracker would be able to follow them from a mile away. Asking her to tone it down wouldn't help. The woman had a square, sturdy, honest chin, but that didn't mean she could take another punch, figuratively speaking. She also had slick blonde hair that darkened at the roots. She was all of five-feet-six-inches tall with an athletic figure. He shouldn't be thinking about her creamy skin, hazel eyes, or full pink lips considering she belonged to his cousin.

Anisa looked like someone famous. He searched his brain for a name and came up empty. Despite belonging to one of the wealthiest cattle ranching families in Texas, his life wasn't a string of parties or events that had him rubbing elbows with Hollywood socialites.

Naturally, when he stopped trying to force it, the name came to him. Sofia Richie. That was who Anisa reminded him of.

Hudson would give it to his cousin. The man had incredible taste in women.

The pregnancy was a shock though. He should probably be used to surprise relationships and babies at this point. There were way more questions than answers with the way Vaughn had treated Anisa. For instance, wouldn't they have kissed before Vaughn took off with that dire warning? He'd said Anisa was his responsibility. Did that mean the child was a surprise? An unwelcomed event? Vaughn didn't seem like he had any animosity toward Anisa. In fact, the word *protective* came to mind.

When Hudson had been trekking for forty solid minutes at a fast clip, he stopped by a dried-up creek bed and turned to Anisa. She was breathing heavy and his heart took a hit that he'd pushed her when she looked so tired. This close, he could see dark circles cradling her eyes. He could only imagine what she'd been through so far or for how long. She must be exhausted even though her chin was out and she looked ready to keep marching if she had to.

One option would be that they could hike to his cabin and get supplies. Based on the fact her clothes had dirt smudges on them and she practically dripped from sweat, he figured a shower and a real bed would go a long way toward making her feel human again.

"How are you?" he asked, not bothering to hide his concern. "Really?"

"I've been better," she said in between breaths. She

leaned forward and grabbed hold of her side as though she had a cramp.

The thought of pushing her farther wasn't exactly warm and fuzzy. They weren't too far from cell phone coverage though. He could make a call and get supplies to them in half an hour if Bronc, the ranch foreman, came blazing. Of course, that might scare away whoever Vaughn was tracking.

"What's really going on?" Hudson asked, wishing he had fresh water to give her.

"You got me," she said, sitting down and leaning her back against a tree trunk. "I was out camping with my brother's ATV when I came upon your cousin. He'd been shot in the thigh and there was so much blood. I couldn't get cell coverage in the area and I couldn't exactly leave him even though he begged me to when he first came to."

"Hold on a minute," Hudson said. "First of all, he was shot?"

"In the thigh. The injury ended up being superficial and I had supplies with me to clean him up and throw in a few stitches," she explained as the cramping seemed to ease.

"Who keeps supplies like that on hand?" he asked, wondering if she was some kind of mercenary in her past life.

"A nurse," she stated. "And your cousin needs to change his bandage in a few hours. He's not the easiest patient but at least he's never yelled at me or cursed me out for helping. He was a trooper when I stitched him up."

Hudson couldn't understand rude people. How hard was it to be nice to someone who was trying to help?

"Thank you for helping Vaughn," Hudson stated, figuring it was never too late to be decent to someone who'd just saved a family member's life.

"You're welcome," she said, her gaze darting toward the ground. Was she embarrassed by the attention?

The second question surfaced. "So, the two of you aren't married?"

The look she gave him caused her entire forehead to wrinkle like she'd just sucked on a sour pickle.

"No," she said. Then, it seemed to click. "Oh. You assumed we were a couple because I'm pregnant and we're together. But he's your cousin. Wouldn't he have told you about a wife and child?"

"I haven't seen or spoken to Vaughn in more years than I care to count," Hudson admitted. "We were close growing up but he signed up for the military the minute we graduated high school. I haven't seen him since."

"And you haven't talked?" she asked.

"We aren't the chatty type," he conceded.

"Is he your only family?" she asked, a concerned wrinkle scoring her forehead.

The question almost brought out a smile.

"Not by a longshot," he quipped, figuring they didn't have enough time to go into the size of his family tree. Right now, the jerk who'd stolen Honey could be closing in on the two of them. "If you're feeling up to it, we should probably stay on the move."

"I'm fine," she said a little too quickly, pushing up to standing. He saw the struggle on her face even though she did her level best to cover.

"We can stay here and rest if you need to," he said calmly, skimming the trees and listening for sounds of hooves.

She shook her head. "I've been hunted, shot at, and nearly killed three times in three days. I need to keep moving until I feel safe again."

Those words hit Hudson square in the chest. He nodded, took her by the hand, and then headed toward a spot he knew had good cell coverage. Once there, he could call the ranch foreman or one of the hands and have a horse and supplies brought nearby.

He walked slower this time. For the time being, the threat seemed to have followed his cousin. He wasn't sure he felt great about the fact, but Vaughn was a trained professional. *One who had been shot,* a little voice in the back of his mind picked that moment to point out. Hudson shelved the thought. He didn't know who was after Vaughn, how, or why. When he saw his cousin again, they needed to talk.

Another forty-five minutes passed. The sun was high overhead, beating down on them both. Lack of food and water would be an issue soon. Hudson had no idea how long a pregnant woman could go without both, but he didn't figure it was too long.

There'd been something haunted in her eyes. Something he couldn't quite pinpoint. Then again, she was on the run. She was trapped in a situation by a sheer stroke of bad luck. She must be exhausted. All he could think was how brave she was being and what a trooper she was to brave the heat and elements in order to save Vaughn. His admiration for her grit and determination grew by the minute. As they neared rougher terrain, he reached for her hand to steady her as they climbed around boulder-sized rocks and through crevices. The second their hands touched, a zing of attraction coursed through him. Hudson hadn't felt anything so powerful in too long. He chalked it up to protective instincts.

His cabin might be the furthest from the main house, but it was the closest to Crater Rock. Could he take her there safely? The location also meant it was most likely the first one someone would come across. Knowing what his cousin was up against would help a whole lot in terms of making better decisions. From what Anisa said, she was an innocent bystander in all this. Keeping her safe until this blew over, or until Vaughn gave the greenlight to return to normal, shouldn't be too difficult. It wasn't like Hudson was moving toward the danger. Vaughn seemed determined to draw the person in the opposite direction of the living quarters. Whoever was after Vaughn probably didn't know about the family. Unless they did. Being a Firebrand could put a target on all of their backs.

Hudson bit back a curse at the thought. There'd been enough chaos at the ranch since the Marshall's accidental death and the crimes that had followed. There was no way he could lead a killer toward home. So, now what?

ANISA BIT back a yawn as Hudson stopped near a clearing. He let go of her hand and she felt another twinge of awareness ripple through her when his gaze caught his. She'd been caught off guard by her body's reaction to the man's touch. But then, she hadn't felt anything nearly close to this since long before Kevin's death. She took it as the first sign her body was finally springing back toward something that resembled normal after being numb for so long.

"I should get cell coverage here," he said. "But I have to get closer to the middle of the field."

She nodded, taking a seat on a downed tree trunk. The sun was bright and had been right overhead for what felt like an eternity but was more likely just the last hour or two. She was hot, tired, and she was pretty sure her deodorant had lost all will to fight against her stink at some point yesterday. The fact Hudson hadn't wrinkled his nose when he got close to her or made a face told her what a gentleman he was.

The first anniversary of her brother's death wasn't supposed to end up like this. Anisa sighed as she watched the only person who knew where they were as he moved out into the open. It would be so much easier for someone with a rifle to pick him off in the field than in the trees. She'd learned that lesson the hard way. Weaving through the trunks had kept her from taking a bullet. And if he got shot now...

Hudson seemed forthright, a comfortingly open presence after Vaughn. Vaughn had been kind, but a complete head scratcher. All he'd said was the people after him wouldn't care about her carrying a child or the fact she was innocent. Now that they'd seen her, they would want her erased. She hadn't been able to have a conversation with him that lasted more than sound bites here and there. They had barely slept, needing to stay on the run. All she knew for certain was there were a couple of men after Vaughn, and—as her luck would have it—now after her. The men had split up at some point during day two and now one was on their heels.

The reason for all of this was still a mystery to her. Vaughn had done something he shouldn't have, to help a friend, but more than that, she had no idea. The persons after them were serious and determined. Vaughn was supposed to be erased.

Erased.

Like in some action movie she would watch at the theater and not here in real life. Her life involved normal things like endless blood pressure checks. She wasn't the high-adrenaline, thrill-ride type. In fact, she'd become a homebody. Most of her days were spent puttering around in the kitchen, binging Netflix, and trying not to eat everything in the fridge since she'd hit her second trimester. Rainy days were meant for reading and she'd picked up baking in recent weeks. Then there was photography. She couldn't say she was especially good at it, but she was gearing up to take pictures of the little one.

Anisa kept one eye on Hudson and the other one on the area surrounding him. Out here, alone and in an unknown area, her chance of survival dipped considerably without him. Add to the fact very real, very scary people were after her and the odds decreased even more. If she couldn't do much else to contribute, the least she could do was keep an eye out. Warn Hudson of anything out of the ordinary as he made the phone call that would hopefully bring a rescue team.

Thankfully, he returned without incident.

"We have a little more hiking to do," he said with an apology. "But we can take it slow."

She winced when she pushed off the tree.

"Is it the baby?" he asked.

"My feet," she said. "I've been on them almost three days straight. They're swollen inside my shoes."

At least she had on decent hiking boots. They were also hot, but they'd kept her feet protected. Little had she known she would need them. She'd worn them for the ATV after reading somewhere that it was best to have on hiking boots.

"We can take a break." He motioned toward the tree where she'd been sitting.

She nodded before returning to the place she'd been a few moments ago. "I'd take these off, but I doubt my feet would fit inside them again."

"Can I ask what you were doing when you found my

cousin?" Hudson shot her a sympathetic look. As much as she should appreciate the compassion, she'd never been one for self-pity. Chin up, she straightened her back.

"You want to know about how I came across your cousin," she stated, figuring he didn't need to hear the details of her life, boring or otherwise.

He gave a quick nod.

"I'd been camping, so I was on my brother's ATV when I stopped to get a drink from my backpack," she explained.

"Forgive my asking, but should a pregnant person be on an ATV?" he asked. One of his sexy dark brows shot up.

"Probably not," she admitted. "It was a special ride and I was taking it easy." She gave a quick glance before looking around for something she could use as a weapon in case one of the men found them. She also realized she was avoiding eye contact with Hudson. It felt as though he could look right through her and see what she was thinking at times since they'd met. "I came across your cousin in a ravine. He needed help so I stopped to render aid. He was in and out of consciousness the first day. I couldn't exactly abandon him and leave him out there to die."

"No cell service, I'm guessing," he said, more of that sympathy shown in his eyes.

"None. You know how it is," she said, figuring he knew better than she. Everything about him screamed outdoor type. He had the kind of rugged good looks and rough hands that came from working for a living. Given he was Vaughn's cousin, he was probably also another Firebrand. The family seemed to have hit the genetic lotto when it came to good looks, honor, and decency.

"Most of the time, it's my favorite part about living out here away from everyone and everything. It's not exactly off the grid at Firebrand Ranch but there's something special about being out here on the land. I don't have to talk to anyone or see anyone if I don't want to," he admitted with a small smile that tugged at her heart.

"It's beautiful here," she agreed, thinking she might like it a whole lot better if she wasn't running for her and her baby's lives.

"We rarely have a need for cell phones," he said. "We all carry, and either ride ATVs or take out our horses. While most cattle ranchers use trucks and ATVs for convenience, and we do some, we grew up doing things the old-fashioned way. Plus, Honey needs the exercise."

"Not everything needs updating. Some things are perfect the way they are," she said, thinking how nice it would be to be able to turn off her cell phone for a few days or ride a horse on beautiful land like this. It was half the appeal of camping.

"So, you just decided to go camping all by yourself?" Hudson continued. He must have a whole lot of questions after the way they'd shown up at the meeting place.

"There was a special reason. I made a promise to someone." She shrugged, not ready to talk about her brother with a stranger. Although, stranger didn't seem quite the right word when thinking about Hudson. When he'd linked their fingers, an electric current had run up her arm. She hadn't felt that kind of electricity with the opposite sex in far too long. She chalked it up to pregnancy hormones or the fact she'd been in mortal danger. Anything but a real connection to a man she'd barely met. "Anyway, it doesn't matter why I was there by myself. Being there is the reason your cousin is on his feet so fast. He would have survived without me as long as the person after him didn't catch up. He seemed to know how to field dress an injury even without store-bought supplies. But he could easily have developed an infection.

This way, he keeps his leg and gets another chance at the bad guy."

"Thank you for what you did for him, by the way," Hudson said. His voice had a low timbre that wrapped around her and through her. "Even though we don't talk every day, and hadn't in years, I never doubt he would have my back and vice versa if need be."

"You came the minute he called," she pointed out. She had no idea what it was like for someone to have her back. She'd been on her own since she was seventeen. In her early twenties, T.J. had located her through social media and asked if she knew where their father was. She'd heard his disappointment come through the line when she'd told him that she had no idea. Her heart had gone out to T.J. The two might not have grown up together, but they were related and he seemed like a genuinely good person. Turned out, T.J.'s mother had died and he was searching for his father to deliver the news. Not that their dad was any prize in the parenting department.

Needing a change of pace, Anisa had packed up her stuff and moved to Austin to be near her half-brother. She and T.J. had become close. Well, as much as was possible. There'd always been a certain distance he'd kept; it was almost as though he couldn't take being let down by a person one more time.

Anisa had recognized the emotion the instant she saw it in T.J. It had been like looking in a mirror.

"Ready to keep moving?" she asked. The temptation to talk to Hudson, to *really* talk to him, had her needing to get going. If she sat there much longer, she might end up spilling her life story.

3

The pregnant woman walking alongside Hudson was a puzzle. She was kind. There was no way she would have stopped to help Vaughn otherwise. She was strong. From what he could tell so far, she'd gone camping for reasons she didn't want to talk about. Anisa didn't strike him as the kind of person who risked her life willy-nilly or ran off halfcocked. There was a story behind the camping trip, and a sadness in her eyes that tugged at his heartstrings. She was intelligent. It was obvious from the first time she opened her mouth. He could go on singing her praises, but he heard the neigh of horses in the distance and the thunder of hooves. Bronc, the ranch foreman, had come through on his promise to have supplies and a horse at the drop spot pronto.

"A little farther," he urged Anisa, checking to make sure she was okay. She walked gingerly on her feet. He couldn't tell how bad the damage was since she had on hiking boots. He could, however, imagine how uncomfortable she must be. Based on her dried, chapped lips, she was also dehydrated.

She nodded and continued.

Luna, Adam's appaloosa, waited along with a backpack filled with food and water. Bronc had been given instructions to stay nearby, watch over the horse and supplies after the drop, then ensure they made it to Hudson's cabin without being followed. Pushing seventy years old, Bronc had more strength and stamina than folks half his age. He was the right person to get the job done no matter what was required. Hudson felt very secure with Bronc at his back.

"We can take a minute to eat and drink some water," he said to Anisa as he surveyed the area and picked up the backpack. He handed a cold bottle of water to her that she immediately pressed to her face and neck.

"This feels good," she said. He noticed her lips first, and the draw to stare at her was strong. He couldn't afford to be distracted by her beautiful face or the delicate lines of her neck. She opened the bottle, downed three-quarters of it, then poured the rest over her face.

"There's more," he said, handing a second bottle over.

She immediately took it and did the exact same thing.

"Looks like there are a few power bars in here," he said, holding out an array on the flat of his palm.

"Peanut butter and chocolate chunks sounds like heaven right now," she said, taking one. She tore open the package and polished off the bar in a matter of a minute.

"Do you want anything else?" He held the bag open to reveal several pieces of fruit.

"I'll take the banana if that's okay," she said. "My legs have been cramping and I must be low on potassium."

"Go for it," he said, taking a certain amount of pleasure in the fact she was getting what she needed.

Anisa finished the banana and then ate an apple before taking a third bottle of water.

"Do you want anything? I feel like I'm taking all the supplies," she said with a look that caused a bomb to detonate inside his chest. There was something lonely about her that connected with the aloneness in him. That was all, he reasoned. The pull toward her wasn't something he needed to focus on.

"I can hold out until we get to my place," he said. "I didn't want you and the baby to starve another minute."

"How far away is your home?" she asked, looking surprised they would be heading there.

"Not far by horseback," he stated.

"I could hug this sweet animal," she said with such relief in her voice that it caused Hudson to smile. Pride welled in his chest that he'd been able to help her out after all she'd done for Vaughn. "But what about your family? What will your wife think of you bringing home a filthy dirty stranger, who also happens to be pregnant?"

"No wife," he said half under his breath. He moved beside Luna, set the bag down, and laced his fingers together. "I can give you a hand up."

Anisa tucked the banana peel inside the pocket of the backpack before placing her boot inside his hand. He hoisted her up easily since she practically weighed nothing. She didn't make eye contact, so he couldn't tell what could possibly be going through her mind. All he did know was that she got quiet after he mentioned his relationship status.

Hudson shouldered the backpack before he mounted, and then settled in behind her.

"Do you ride?" he asked.

"Not really," she said with a slight shrug.

This way, he had to wrap his arms around her in order to hold tight to the reins. A fission of electricity rocketed through him as he circled her waist. The live wire feeling in the pit of his stomach was getting harder to ignore. He chalked it up to protective instincts for a pregnant woman in danger and moved on.

The ride to his cabin took longer than usual, but he had no plans to cantor Luna. Hudson didn't know much about babies or pregnancy, but he sure didn't want her little one bouncing out before it was fully cooked.

"Let's get you inside and off your feet," he said to Anisa once he'd dismounted and tied Luna off. Bronc would swing by and pick her up once Hudson's 'cargo' was safely inside. He didn't want Bronc to see her or have a description. The less anyone knew, the better. In fact, Hudson had no plans to keep her here at the ranch. She needed a break and to catch her breath, and then he could drive them both to a nearby hotel, maybe a couple of towns over or closer toward Houston. The bigger the city, the better. Folks didn't notice each other much in crowded places. In Lone Star Pass, she would be the talk of the town if he tried to stick around.

"I'd love a shower and clean clothes," she said as he helped her off Luna. "A toothbrush would be heaven."

"I have all those things inside," he said, noticing how her slightest smile drew him closer to her like she had a secret meant for his ears only. She didn't. And yet he couldn't deny the mental connection they shared. They were like two old souls who finally found each other after searching for several lifetimes.

Anisa climbed down.

"Feel free to go on inside," he said, stepping to one side. He wanted to brief Bronc on the situation and keep a watch out for Vaughn in case his cousin doubled back to join them at the cabin and he needed to check to see if Honey had been spotted or, by some miracle, had returned.

"Are you forgetting something?" she asked, one of those eyebrows arched.

He looked down and around before bringing his gaze back up to meet hers. He shrugged. "Not that I can see."

She blinked at him.

"Key?" she asked but it was more statement than question.

"It's not locked," he responded. "We don't normally have crime here around the living areas of the ranch." Although, he should probably change his habit after the wave that seemed to strike the ranch in recent months. Old habits were hard to change.

"Do you leave your key inside your vehicle, as well?" she asked as she started past him with more than a little surprise in her tone.

"Yes," he said without ceremony. He should probably stop doing that too. "Make yourself comfortable. The layout is easy to figure out. Guest bathroom is always stocked."

"I will," she said as she paused long enough to reach for the door handle. "And thank you."

"Leave your clothes in the hallway if you want 'em washed. There should be a clean robe in the bathroom you can use," he stated. All Hudson wondered was why the sound of her voice filled some of that hole in his chest. He'd only just met her, barely knew her, and she was most likely in a long-term relationship. Or at the very least was committed to someone else.

"Oh. Okay," she said, sounding more than a little surprised at the offer. He didn't get the impression she was used to being on the receiving end of help. She also had a stubborn chin and determined, if momentarily defeated, eyes. Those hazel eyes had a terra-cotta colored base with flecks of golds, greens, and browns in the center. He'd met very few with their equal. Hazel eyes were as rare as someone like Anisa. And she was probably taken, he reminded. Just because she didn't wear a gold band didn't mean she wasn't married. Signs might be pointing to her being single but they could be misleading if read out of context. Going camping alone while pregnant seemed risky for someone who seemed to calculate her moves with great care. She'd alluded to the fact the trip had a special meaning. His mind reeled with possibilities. None he liked or wished on someone as decent and kind as Anisa. Because the lost quality to her eyes despite her show of strength pointed his thoughts to a tragedy, and she didn't deserve that.

ANISA HOBBLED inside the one-story cabin. The open-concept space was light and airy with high ceilings and walls of windows facing the back of the property. The décor was masculine without giving off a frat house vibe. A metal star hung over the tumbled stone fireplace, the mantel a solid piece of wood. Twin leather sofas that looked ready to sink into flanked the room. There were end tables that looked made from driftwood and an oversized leather ottoman covered with a tray on top. The dining room and kitchen meshed into one space and there was an oversized granite island as the only room separation. There was a hallway to her left and one to her right.

She sat down on the bench by the door and peeled off her hiking boots. She tucked her socks inside, wrinkling her nose at the smell of both. Since she didn't want to be a bad guest and cause his entire living area to stink, she cracked the door open and set both on the porch out front.

Now that she was indoors, she could smell her own body odor full force. The term *ripe* didn't quite do it justice. She wrinkled her nose and developed a whole new appreciation for what a gentleman Hudson was. It was probably owing to the cowboy code he seemed to live by.

The guest wing was in the hallway to the right of the living space. She couldn't get to the shower fast enough. Peeling off the clothes, she put them inside the empty trash can and slid it into the hallway. Her feet were in better shape than she first realized, so that was a small win. A little compression and then ice should help with the swelling. The cold water in the shower would help too.

Twenty minutes later, Anisa was showered, teeth brushed, and in the softest robe she'd probably ever felt in her life. She rubbed her belly. "Are you okay in there?"

The pregnancy had shocked her to say the least. But now she'd grown attached to the little bean that was growing inside her. Worry crept in that the little person was so quiet. Maybe the bean was in energy conservation mode? If the baby didn't move soon, she would reach out to her doctor just to be certain everything was okay. A career in nursing had given her nerves of steel and, more importantly, patience.

Anisa joined Hudson in the kitchen. His hair was wet from a shower. She ignored the droplets of water rolling down his neck. He had on a simple outfit of a t-shirt and jeans. The white cotton stretched across a muscled chest. The denim hung low on his hips where his body formed an improbable V. The rancher had the kind of looks and body that could easily have him confused for an underwear model who should be on a billboard in Times Square.

And yet, he'd proven to be one of the most down to earth people she'd met in a long time. Ever?

"What's that heavenly smell?" She took in a deep breath, forcing her gaze away from his chest where it didn't belong.

"Make yourself comfortable on the couch," he said. "I'll bring food over your way and more water."

Anisa did as requested, not minding being spoiled for a minute. She was already starting to rehydrate and the lip balm she'd put on her lips after brushing was going a long way toward healing her chapped lips. She would collect her things, find transportation, and get out of his hair after she iced her feet. The quickest way to remove the threat would be to take herself out of the equation.

"I know I already thanked you, but I want you to know how much I appreciate everything you're doing for me," she said. "I also realize this is a favor for your cousin and not me personally but that doesn't mean I appreciate it any less."

"You're welcome and I would have helped anyway if I'd found you out on my family's land," he said without missing a beat as he set a tray down on the coffee table then pushed it beside the couch. "It's just the way we do things out here."

"Well, it's above and beyond the call of duty, if you ask me," she said, thinking she didn't know a whole lot of people who would drop everything and go to the lengths he had without any explanation whatsoever. It was foreign to Anisa for someone to be so kind and caring, and a nice change of pace to be able to rely on someone else. She'd been on her own growing up and the death of her half-brother meant she was all alone in the world. But then, she'd always relied on herself. Even T.J. had his limits when it came to family relationships.

Hudson waved her off like it was nothing, but he'd already reached sainthood in her book.

"There's more than one person hunting your cousin,"

she said as she picked up the plate of spaghetti and meatballs. The smell alone made her mouth water.

"How many?" he asked.

"At least two," she said. "But that doesn't mean there aren't more."

Hudson nodded. His lips formed a grim line and she could see worry stamped all over otherwise perfect features. Her chest squeezed and she refocused on the meal in front of her.

She took a bite and the taste was even better than the smell. "This is amazing."

"I can't take credit," he said, putting his hands up in the surrender position, palms out. He fixed a plate for himself and then joined her, sitting on the opposite couch and balancing a tray on his knees.

Anisa didn't say another word until her plate was clean. There was something comforting about the meal, like it had been prepared by a grandmother she'd never known who was looking down on her, watching over her, ensuring the little bean was gaining energy and strength. Going with little more than power bars to keep her going over the past few days had her worried whether or not the baby was getting enough nutrition. "I can't remember the last time I ate something this amazing."

"My mom will be thrilled. It's her special recipe. She's been making these since I was a kid. Never gets old," he said with more than a hint of appreciation.

"I'd give her a hug if I could," she quipped as she set the plate down on the tray next to her. A moment later, the coffee table was back in its original position. She tried to rub her aching feet. "Has she ever thought of opening a restaurant?"

He laughed and the sound bathed her in warmth and light.

"She should probably get paid for all the mouths she's fed, but, no, she would never consider doing it for a living. She said it might take the joy out of the process if she was forced to meet a quota every day," he said.

"Smart woman," Anisa quipped. "I had a romantic idea about becoming a nurse. I pictured myself spending my days being a superhero, swooping in and giving comfort to the sick." She laughed. "Little did I realize the job would include so many bodily fluids ending up on my scrubs." She shivered at the thought of the last kid who threw up on her. "I had a kid who literally hit me from across the room. Gave the word projectile a whole new meaning."

Hudson's smile didn't reach his eyes. His amusement seemed tempered by his concern for Vaughn. She completely understood and wished there was something she could do for him.

"What else do you need?" he asked.

"Finish eating first," she said, thinking he was more concerned with others than himself. There was something comfortable and casual about being here after what she'd been through. She shouldn't feel so safe in a stranger's home. Exhaustion was also taking hold so that could be playing a part. She scanned the fireplace mantel and then the end tables for pictures of Hudson with a woman. Curiosity was getting the best of her and she wanted to know more about him and his personal life.

The place had a distinct bachelor vibe and looked like the kind of place a person lived who could pick up after himself. The fact he was taking care of her and seemed to be able to handle chores like laundry impressed her. Mainly because, from what little she knew about the Firebrands, they had money to spare. Shouldn't they have servants waiting on them hand and foot? She pictured that old TV show *Dallas*. This place was nothing like the J.R. and Bobby Ewing.

"Done." Hudson made a show of ensuring she could see his empty plate. "Now, what can I do for you?"

"I need something to wrap my feet in. Any kind of gauze will do if you have some," she said. "Then, I'll need a bucket filled with ice."

"Compression and then ice. Got it," he said. He stood up and collected trays before disappearing into the opposite hallway. It was almost a shame she couldn't stay here overnight to rest. At least she was still technically on vacation and didn't have to worry about calling in sick for work, or worse yet showing up and explaining how she'd ended up in this condition. Although, she wouldn't call the camping trip a vacation by any stretch of the imagination. She had no idea what her brother saw in sleeping outside. She would give him the incredible sky part. The first night, it had looked like a blanket of velvet with brilliant sparks of light as far as the eye could see. Magical wasn't nearly strong enough a word to describe a sky that looked part fairy tale and part mystical.

She'd lived in Austin five years now and hadn't stopped to go outside at night long enough to stare at the stars. Of course, she'd been working and putting herself through nursing school, which meant dinner in front of the TV of her small apartment and then being zonked out before ten at night.

Hudson returned with the requested supplies and then said, "Will you allow me to do the honors?"

More of that curiosity had her nodding before her mouth could say the words *no thanks*. The thought of him taking care of her sent warmth like a campfire on a freezing cold night spreading through her. Her chest squeezed as he kneeled down next to her and her breath caught the second he reached for her ankle. Frissons of heat swirled up her leg at contact. Anisa tried to shake off her body's reaction to the strong man near her but was helpless against the onslaught.

4

Hudson had wrapped more injuries than he could count over the years and figured it might be easier for him to take charge rather than have her struggle to do it for herself. Based on her reactions to his offers of help, he got the distinct impression she was used to taking care of herself. As much as he admired the trait, he understood how difficult it could be to accept a hand up from others when needed. He had a niggling feeling she wouldn't be so cooperative if she hadn't been pregnant. And yet his heart still pounded wildly in his chest since the moment she accepted his offer of help.

"Mind if I ask where you're from?" he asked, figuring small talk might make the time pass faster. He still hadn't heard a word from Vaughn, and Bronc had already alerted the family and to the threat on the property. Since trying to help Vaughn could make matters worse, Hudson asked Bronc to pass the word that they should stand down for the time being. So there was literally nothing left for them to do, other than wait.

"I live in Austin but I'm from Denver originally," she said.

"Decided you didn't like the snow?" he asked. He couldn't think of two more different weather patterns.

"The mountains are pretty enough," she said on a noncommittal shrug. "Guess I'm not a cold weather person."

"Give me sunshine any day over the white stuff," he agreed, taking care in wrapping her feet as he held her ankle in the palm of his hand.

"I came here to be closer to family about five years ago," she said after a long pause. The break in conversation had been so long Hudson half figured she was done talking.

"Family is important," he said, wondering if he was making the right move to ditch his and start the taco business. Austin had come to mind as one of the cities he'd been serious about. "I've been thinking of making a move away from mine."

"You don't get along?" she asked.

"It's complicated; I have a great mother and I couldn't love my brothers any more than I do. But we've had a rift in the family and it's tearing us and our cousins apart," he said, surprised he was so willing to talk about what had been happening. Although, to be fair, it was nice to be able to speak to someone who had no skin in the game. Anisa was an objective outsider. "My father and uncle are gasoline on fire."

"That's too bad," she said, looking around his cabin in what looked a lot like unabashed awe. "If I lived in a place like this, wild horses couldn't drag me away."

Well, that made Hudson smile. It was good to see the place from an outsider's perspective.

"It was an amazing place to grow up," he said.

"I can imagine," she said off the cuff. "How many brothers did you say you had?"

"Eight," he said as he secured the gauze on her right foot.

"Are you kidding me right now?" she asked, the sound of shock in her voice made him chuckle.

"Nine sons including myself," he added.

"I can scarcely imagine taking care of one." She rubbed her belly and he wondered if the move was subconscious.

She gave his work a good once-over after quickly regaining her composure.

"That's a great job you're doing," she said, admiring his work. "I'm impressed."

"Living on a ranch, you learn to do things for yourself," he admitted before getting to work on the left. It didn't take long for him to finish the job and his chest puffed with pride that he'd been useful to her. "There you go."

"My feet feel better already," she said with a smile that caused a knife stab to the center of his chest.

Hudson moved to the opposite couch since being close to her had him wanting to reveal all his secrets. Space didn't help as much as he'd hoped.

"How many siblings do you have?" he asked, figuring he could turn the tables to avoid boring her with the details of his life.

"One," she said with a palpable sadness she was trying to cover by taking a sip of bottled water. "But he's gone now."

"I'm really sorry. I didn't mean to bring up a sore subject," he started but she stopped him with a hand up.

"Don't be. It's a reasonable question. He's been gone for a year now and I never talk about him," she said. "T.J. was his name and he was my half-brother. I moved here when his mother died. He is...*was*...a few years younger than me and tracked me down over social media. He just sounded so alone when he called, asking if I knew where our father was. He was barely out of his teens."

"That's too young to lose a parent," he said, hating that she'd gone through it.

"It was. And to be left with just our father...though my mom wasn't much better. It seems our dad had a way of picking them." She rolled her eyes. "But you don't want to hear about my family drama."

"I don't mind," he quickly countered. "Believe me when I say there isn't much you could say or do to shock me."

"You'd be surprised," she said with conviction that caught him off guard.

"What happened to your brother?" he asked, hoping he wasn't pushing a hurtful topic.

"He had a bad accident that did a lot of emotional damage. He lost the ability to walk and couldn't seem to recover emotionally afterward. He became addicted to pain killers and then depressed," she said, stopping there. Suddenly, the rim of the water bottle became very interesting and her voice cracked as she said those last words. The writing was on the wall. Either the injuries caught up with him or the kid had taken his own life.

"I can only imagine how awful that was for you to go through," he said and meant it. "I wish there was something I could do."

"It's been a year. The ATV was his. He asked me to take it out every year and go camping with it in his honor." Anisa's smile didn't reach her eyes when she thanked him for his kindness. "Believe it or not, talking about T.J. with you is the first time..." She paused like she needed a minute. Then, she blinked her eyes a couple of times and focused on her feet. "You know, you could be a nurse."

Other questions popped into Hudson's mind. What about the baby's father? Where was he? As much as he wanted to know more about her situation, he knew better than to ask. She'd changed the subject. She wanted to move on.

He could only imagine how horrific it would be to lose a brother, especially one so young. He'd had his whole life ahead of him and should have be planning his future. He would have been an uncle soon and Hudson figured half the reason Anisa had moved to Austin five years ago was to hold onto the only family she knew. Hearing about her problems made his seem small by comparison. It also made him want to send a note to his brothers telling them how much he loved each one of them and appreciated how much any one of them would be there for him in a heartbeat. Having a large family to back him had always been a perk of being a Firebrand.

"I know I've been talking for twenty minutes straight," she said, and her cheeks flamed. The washing machine picked that moment to chime in to let him know the load was ready to go into the dryer.

"Hold on," he said before disappearing into the next room to move clothes. His heart went out to Anisa. Hearing about her brother had practically gutted him. She hadn't mentioned a boyfriend or husband. Wouldn't she have by now if there was one?

Hudson filled a bucket with ice from a bag in the freezer outside in the garage. He brought it to Anisa and set it down next to the sofa. "Do you like ice cream?"

"Is that a serious question?" She unwrapped her feet, one at a time, before easing them into the ice bucket. "It's so cold but I know it's going to make my feet feel amazing when I'm done."

"Compression and ice are a high school athlete's best friend," he joked, figuring she needed a little levity after sharing something so personal. Besides, from somewhere deep within he wanted to see her smile.

"And ice cream makes almost everything better," she quipped with a smile that caused his throat to dry up. The trick was going to be taking care of Anisa without falling for her. Because his heart seemed to be going down a surprising path when it came to the mystery nurse.

IT WAS AMAZING WHAT A SHOWER, clean clothes, and a full stomach could do for the spirits. Not to mention the fact a strong rancher seemed intent on making Anisa as comfortable as possible. The ice cream had been an unexpected touch. The soft couch was beyond a luxury at this point. After taking care of her feet, while eating ice cream, Anisa leaned back and rested her eyes whilst Hudson took care of the dishes. There was something incredibly sexy about a self-sufficient man. There'd been too few of those in Anisa's life up to this point. This was the first time in the last few days when she felt a little safe and like she could let her guard down for a second and not be shot at or startled awake by an animal.

A loud noise surprised her. She sat bolt upright, opening her eyes against the dimly lit room. It took a few seconds for her eyes to adjust, considering it had been broad daylight the last time she recalled being awake.

"I didn't want to wake you," Hudson's gravelly voice rolled over her and through her, stirring places she'd forgotten existed inside her. An overwhelming sense of calm washed over her, like his presence would somehow make the world all right again. Anisa shook it off.

He sat up, yawned, and rubbed his eyes. Good looks were one thing in a person, superficial. Anisa didn't get caught up in the trap of falling for the shell. She cared about what was happening on the inside. It was interesting how an attractive person could become ugly really fast once they opened their mouth to speak, and vice versa.

"What was that noise?" she asked.

His smile happened at the exact moment it occurred to her what had happened. She'd snored herself awake.

"Never mind," she said, embarrassment heating her cheeks. At least it was too dark for him to see how mortified she was. "I just figured it out."

"Don't worry about it," he said like it was nothing. "You should see me during calving season." He chuckled and it was a low rumble in his chest. The man's sexy sleepy voice could turn on a rock.

"What's that?" she asked, more heat flaming her cheeks that she tried her best to ignore. This time, it had nothing to do with embarrassment and everything to do with the warmth circling in her body. Being near Hudson was the equivalent of stumbling on a campfire on a freezing cold night. She was drawn to him. It made sense. He'd literally just saved her life, given her comforts. The whole knight-in-shining-armor applied. Her pregnancy hormones heightened everything too. Her reaction to Hudson made sense when she really broke it down logically.

"That's baby season at the ranch. It begins in February and runs a couple of months until the last one is born. Ranchers get basically no sleep during that point in time," he said.

"Why February? Can't cows reproduce any other time?" she asked.

"February-born calves are generally older and heavier when weaned; and they're all weaned in October. We aim for sixty percent of our calves to be born in the first thirty days of the season," he explained before catching her gaze. "Do you drink coffee?"

"I used to," she practically groaned. Her hand instinctively went to her belly. "I'm taking a hiatus for the time being."

"A mother's sacrifice never ceases to amaze me," he responded, causing more of that Hudson-esque warmth to roll through her. He stood up and walked toward the kitchen. "Will it bother you if I have a cup?"

"Knock yourself out," she quipped, thinking she probably wouldn't have bothered to ask if the shoe was on the other foot. Giving up caffeine had been the most difficult part of the pregnancy so far. She'd been lucky and had only had mild symptoms in the first trimester. She had no intention of tempting fate.

She pushed up to standing so she could stretch. Her feet were in surprisingly good shape after the treatment yesterday. She extended her arms out with a yawn. Her lips were already better. She needed to write down the name of the lip balm in the bathroom because it had worked a miracle.

In general terms, she was in great shape. They'd lost her belongings and most of their supplies on the second morning, so she hadn't gone long without proper hydration. They'd avoided the sun as best as possible too.

She could use a bathroom and some water. Maybe breakfast. The baby made her eat every few hours usually.

Anisa rubbed her small bean again, wishing the little one would move. When nothing happened, she excused herself and headed toward the guest bathroom. After freshening up, she returned to the living area to find her clothes folded and stacked on the coffee table.

"In case you want to get dressed," he said as the smell of fresh-brewed coffee wafted by. She'd never been one of those pregnant people who suddenly got sick at certain smells. Fluctuating hormones had been a whole different story. She'd cry at the drop of a pin. But then, there was a very different reason for that in the first trimester. There'd been so much grief that she didn't even realize she'd missed her period, and hers had usually been like clockwork.

"I would like that very much," she responded, picking up the clothing. Standing up straight made her a little lightheaded. She saw a few stars. Nothing unusual.

Clean clothes made her feel all the way human again. Her feet screamed that they didn't want to look at those hiking boots again, but being in tight shoes that covered her ankles had probably saved her from even more swelling. Plus, she didn't need to wear shoes in the house anyway, but when she finally got home she was investing in the fluffiest pair of slippers that she could find.

When she returned to the kitchen this time, she smelled oatmeal, cinnamon, and toast with butter. She was practically salivating by the time she sat down at the granite island.

"It isn't fancy, but should do the trick," he said by way of explanation.

Little did he know, she could kiss him for the meal. The thought shocked her. She didn't need to fall down the rabbit hole of attraction with this sexy cowboy. Her feelings toward him were most likely a reaction to him saving her life. Her body's reaction to the man was for obvious reasons. He was smokin' hot with a bod made for sinning. His character drew her in even more and made her want to get to know him. It was probably best if she tried to maintain an emotional distance from here on out.

"This is perfect. My stomach could use a good bowl of oatmeal. It's my comfort food, actually," she said.

"Mine too," he said with a slight smile. One that tugged at her heart despite her resolve not to let Hudson Firebrand affect her anymore.

"It's warm and calming and gentle on the stomach," she continued, practically mewling with pleasure after the first bite.

"Taste okay?" he asked after he took a sip of coffee.

"Are you kidding? This is heaven," she managed to get out in between bites. At this point, she couldn't care about the impression she gave off by chowing down. The little bean could be demanding when meals had been denied.

It was still dark outside. She glanced at the clock in the kitchen. "I didn't realize it was four-thirty."

"Middle of the night for most folks," he said.

"Why do you look so awake?" she asked, and then realized he was probably still waiting for word about Vaughn.

"I wake up around four every day," he supplied. "Usually get in a small workout before coffee."

"Interesting. I didn't realize ranchers and nurses had anything in common," she said.

He shot her a quizzical look.

"I'm on the six a.m. shift change, which means I have to arrive at work at five-thirty if I don't want to get cursed out by the shift leader," she explained.

"Speaking of work," he started. "Do you need to call in?"

"I'm still on vacation," she said.

"What about a husband or boyfriend?" he asked, and

she thought there was something in his voice when he asked, which was probably just her imagination.

Right?

For a long moment Anisa debated whether or not it was a good idea to respond to his question. She mentally shook her head, rejecting the idea. It was too sad to talk about Kevin. Too confusing. And brought up too many conflicting feelings about the way he'd spent his last day on earth. No, Anisa couldn't go there. Not right now.

5

"Have you heard word on Vaughn?" Anisa's hazel eyes widened with the question.

Hudson shook his head and compressed his lips. He realized she'd just changed the subject but decided not to press for details. Besides, the lack of contact with Vaughn had been gnawing at the back of his mind. A knot had formed in his chest too. But he took note of the fact Anisa hadn't answered his question as to whether or not there was a boyfriend or husband in the picture. Touchy subject? It wasn't his business, so he let it go no matter how much his curiosity was getting the best of him.

"He has a tendency to hide in places there probably isn't cell coverage. He said it keeps an enemy from communicating with others in case there's more than one person," she explained, her tone gentle.

"I have no doubt his years in the military have kicked in," Hudson stated, thinking their experience with tracking poachers on the ranch had set them up for just such a scenario. "Did he give you any indication of who might be after him?"

"He mainly just apologized. He mumbled something about no good deed going unpunished at one point, but when I asked what he meant by that, he didn't respond," she said.

"What is your overall impression of the situation? You spent a couple of days with my cousin." She'd spent more time with Vaughn in the past couple of days than Hudson or anyone else from the family had in a decade. Hudson had no idea how much the military, not to mention time and age, had changed his former best friend.

"Whoever is after him seems to think like he does," she said after a thoughtful pause.

"Do you mean like military or survival skills?" he asked.

"Definitely military," she said. "I got the impression Vaughn was very good at his job in the service. The fact this person was able to keep up with us frustrated him to no end."

"I can't imagine someone who'd taken a survival boot-camp could measure up to Vaughn, especially considering he grew up on a ranch where there were poachers to keep watch for. We all learned how to track at a young age. Then, there was gun training. Since there have always been weapons around, we were taught at an early age how to respect them. Vaughn was probably the best shooter in the family," he said. "He was a top tracker as well."

"Now, some of his mumblings make more sense," she said. "He would say random words when he was sleeping, especially the first night." She paused for a long beat and the smile faded from her lips at the memory. "I'll be one hundred percent honest with you. At first, I thought he was running from the law. In my mind, he was a criminal who'd been shot while escaping and could be dangerous."

"And yet you helped him anyway," Hudson said.

"I signed up to heal the sick, not judge them," she stated with a shrug. "Besides, he was in no condition to fight me if push came to shove. I could have outrun him on the first night and my conscience would have been clean because I would have at least tried. Once he got stitched and some medicine on his wounds, he started healing quickly. He's in top physical condition, so I had no doubts that once he was up and running he would do fine. I kept his backpack out of reach the first night too. Just in case he had a weapon in there. Plus, there was no reason to upset me or threaten me. I was already helping and he seemed grateful straight out of the gate."

"He was lucky you came up on him when you did," Hudson said. He didn't want to consider the possibilities if she hadn't found Vaughn. Although, he had a feeling Vaughn would have figured out a way to land on his feet. At least Hudson hoped it was true. But what could his cousin have gotten himself into in the short time since he'd left the military? That was the question.

"We both got lucky if you ask me," she said. "I realize he doesn't believe this, or at least that's what he said. However, I was alone camping on private property. I didn't realize it at the time but I'm guessing I ended up trespassing on your land."

"That's not hard to do in these parts," he quipped. It was true. His family owned much of what the eye could see north of town, and well beyond the Texan border.

"I quickly realized Vaughn was a good person," she said. "Years of nursing experience and dealing directly with the public helps you develop a sense about people when you meet them."

"Working a ranch is the same way. We get transient

workers and it becomes easier to tell the good ones from the bad ones. Bronc, our foreman, taught me early on to look in the eyes," he said. "It's impossible to hide pure evil when you look in someone's eyes."

"I was just about to say the same thing," she said, her hazels lit up when she spoke. Hers were an incredible mix of brown, yellow, and green against pure white. The contrast was striking. She issued a sharp sigh and said, "I should probably get going. Is there any way I can leave my contact information? I'd like to know that Vaughn is okay when you find him." She glanced around and then smacked her forehead. "I lost my backpack out there. I have no ID, keys, or money. Any chance I can borrow enough to get home?"

"Where's home?" he asked, figuring he could do a whole lot better than that.

"Austin," she supplied.

"I'd be happy to drive you there myself," he said. He had an ulterior motive. He needed to make sure the coast was clear at her place. His conscience wouldn't be able to stand dropping her off and then finding out something awful happened to her. "Word of caution, though."

Her eyebrows knitted together as she tilted her head to one side. He'd noticed her do this earlier when she was confused. The move was adorable in a way that wouldn't be sexy on any other person.

"The person after Vaughn might have found your backpack," he stated. "And we can't exactly retrace your steps. Not safely, and not without Vaughn's green light. The last thing I would want to do is make whatever he's doing more difficult."

"I hadn't thought about the backpack," she admitted, her chest deflating as she blew out a breath. "It would give the person who was after us all my information. My home address. Cell phone. If this person happened to have connections or military-level experience they could hack into my phone and get all my personal data."

Hudson nodded.

"At the very least, you need to call your provider and cancel your service so no one can rack up charges," he said.

"And I need to mark my phone as lost with Apple too. As well as figure out if I can do the same thing with my ID. Do you have a laptop I can use?" she asked. Tension lines scored her forehead. "And a phone I can use to call my service provider?"

Hudson grabbed his laptop from the small office next to his bedroom after handing over his cell. "If you have the number of any of your neighbors, you might want to give them a call to see if anyone suspicious has been around your place."

"I wish I did. I've only lived in my current place for six months. My fiancé and I were supposed to move in together there but—"

She stopped midsentence and shot him a look. There was something behind her eyes, a mix of sadness and regret, that was another stab to the chest. His mind started rolling over possible scenarios. The guy freaked once he found out she was pregnant. They broke up before she could tell him she was carrying his child. The guy still didn't know about the child.

"Did he know about the baby?" Hudson asked, knowing full well it wasn't any of his business. The question came out before he had a chance to reel it back in. "Sorry. You don't have to answer that."

"No," she said with more than a hint of sadness in her voice that took his mind down a different path. Hudson fisted his hands to stop them from reaching out to comfort her, even though he had no idea what he would be comforting her about. "He didn't."

There was something else in her tone that told him to back off the subject for now. Hudson's radar was up and he wanted to know what had happened or if he could help in some way. Anisa would tell him more when she was good and ready, even though more questions immediately formed in his mind.

"Here's the laptop," he said, taking the seat next to her. He opened it and hit the power button. After entering the password, he positioned the screen toward her so she could access the keyboard. Their hands incidentally touched and more of that electricity vibrated through him.

It took an hour for Anisa to handle her phone situation, and another ten for her to block access to her credit card.

"Thankfully, I cleaned out my wallet before the trip. I figured that I only needed my ID and one credit card," she said.

"It's good to be grateful for small miracles," he said.

"According to the website, I need to go to a police station to report my license as stolen or missing," she stated.

"That's tricky right now," he said.

"I know. I don't want to draw attention to Vaughn," she reasoned.

This incredible woman had lost the brother she loved, possibly a fiancé, and was bringing a life into the world, presumably on her own. No one person deserved to have all that heaped on her, especially not one as kind and giving as Anisa. She could have easily walked away from Vaughn and gotten as far away from him as possible. She could have forgotten she'd seen him. But she didn't.

She just didn't seem to be built that way.

ANISA RAN through all the ways in which the person who had her backpack could make her life miserable. There was, of course, a possibility that no one had it. The patchwork job she'd picked up at a fair might still be out on the property somewhere, all on its lonesome. Was that too good to hope for?

She needed to plan for the worst even as she hoped for the best. Then, if by some miracle, the backpack was recovered along with her personal information and items, she could relax. Until then, she had to assume it had been found or would be. It also occurred to her that Hudson had lost something very valuable to him as well.

"Have you heard anything about Honey?" she quickly asked.

"She's back in the barn. Bronc came across her as she neared the clearing, heading toward the barn last night," he said with a look of pride. It was easy to see he cared a great deal for his horse. "She's been trained to head back home if we get separated. I just wasn't sure if she was in trouble and able to make the journey." His vehicle was back at the main house since he'd ridden a golf cart to the barn as he often did.

"What a relief," she said, unable to imagine how awful it must have been in those few hours her whereabouts were unknown.

"She's fine, so that's one big win out of this situation," he stated. He clenched his back teeth and she saw the tension still working its way out of his system.

Anisa had the same thought about this being a win though. Considering how the past few days had gone, she'd take all the positive news she could get. Facing her brother's birthday had kept her in a bad mood for weeks leading up to it. She'd hoped to get some relief by taking out the ATV like he'd asked. But doing so alone had only served to make her feel even lonelier.

Any hope the open air and beautiful scenery would clear her mind and offer some sense of peace was dashed on her first night when she just sat and cried. Anisa was so not a crier. Normally, she had to watch a movie like *Black Beauty* or *Hachi* to get tears flowing. Precisely why she'd successfully avoided watching *Marley and Me* up to this point.

It suddenly occurred to her that she might want to call her obstetrician and ask about the lack of movement from the little bean. Logically, she knew everything was probably fine. While she had been under duress, she'd been careful to stay hydrated when they had access to water. She hadn't been without long enough to cause concern. Still, the lack of movement was bothering her.

Most often times, new mothers overreacted over the slightest things. It was common and understandable. The job was big and the body underwent many changes in a short time to accommodate a baby. Being a nurse had hardened her in some ways. She figured most stuff would work itself out. She didn't call her obstetrician outside of office hours because she also realized if something bad happened to the pregnancy, there wasn't much that could be done. Unless there was bleeding, cramping, or discharge, she knew nature would step up and take care of the rest. There was usually no reason for panic.

She glanced up at Hudson only to realize he was studying her.

"You seem like the kind of person who already has a plan for how the day should go," she said with a small smile.

"I have some ideas that I'd like to run past you," he said,

returning the smile. The man was even more beautiful when he smiled.

Anisa had to suppress a laugh. A man like Hudson would scoff at being called beautiful. But he was. Not in a polished, professional manner. His good looks and sex appeal came from his rugged good looks and his eyes. He was right about the eyes. They revealed a whole lot about a person. And his were like looking into a pure pool. There was so much honesty and kindness there. He had a boyish charm but could take care of himself. It was easy to forget the fact the man was from a prominent Texas family. Nothing about him said spoiled or indulged. He was one of the most down-to-earth types she'd ever met, which was unexpected given his social stature.

Maybe those qualities came with being a rancher. His rough hands revealed he knew a hard day's work. His body looked sculpted, like he'd just come from the gym but she knew better. His had come from working the family business.

"Go for it," she said.

"I thought we might head over to Austin when you were finished here. We could circle around your place and get the lay of the land since you don't know your neighbors. I'd like to check the place out make sure it hasn't been set on fire," he said.

Anisa gasped even though he wasn't being literal. The thought of losing what little she'd worked and scrimped for sent her pulse racing. She reminded herself stress wasn't good for the baby. Instinctively, she dropped her hands to her stomach and cradled the little bean.

And then she felt it. The baby moved. A wave of relief washed over her, tumbling through her. She could barely contain the emotions that had been bottled up and were trying to get the best of her. "Do you mind holding on a minute?"

"What is it?" Hudson asked, concern wrinkling his forehead.

"The bean moved," she said as reality struck the baby was moving and, therefore, would be all right. Tears pricked the backs of her eyes at the first sign of hope something in this situation might work out. "This little person has been still, too still, and I was starting to worry that..." Anisa suppressed the urge to cry. It was habit by now ingrained in her from a long life of holding in her emotions. She had enough practice to make the pro leagues at this point, if such a thing existed.

"I'm sorry," Hudson said. "I had no idea you've been concerned."

"No. It's not your fault," she quickly said. "I didn't want to make a big deal out of it until I knew for certain what was going on. The baby might have been moving when I was napping or just being quiet. Being a nurse teaches you to take most things with a grain of salt. I generally fall into the wait-and-see camp, but it was starting to take too long and now it's okay, so..." She paused long enough to take a couple of slow breaths. "I'm just relieved everything is back on track."

"That's good news," Hudson said and his voice soothed more parts of her that she'd buried. "We need more of that right now."

She nodded and smiled, allowing herself this small win. "You were saying something before..."

"I had a question, actually. You don't like the idea of a slow approach to your place?" he asked and some of his tension lines had eased too.

"Oh no. It's not that. It's a solid plan," she said.

"Don't get too agreeable. You haven't heard all of it yet," he warned.

"Okay. What else?" she asked, arching an eyebrow.

"I'd like to stick around until we hear from Vaughn," he said and his voice was tentative. He clearly was expecting pushback on this point, or afraid he'd crossed a line.

"Okay," she responded.

He opened his mouth to speak like he was about to mount an argument and then clamped it shut. "Wait a second. You said, 'Okay.'"

"If it was just my life on the line, I would probably be more stubborn about it. I've always liked my privacy and I've been taking care of myself for a very long time. But this is different," she reasoned. "This is protecting my baby and I'm not at full speed. The past couple of days has brought home that point very clearly."

"Good," he said. "I mean, not good that you don't feel capable of handling yourself, but good that you're willing to accept my help. Thank you."

Anisa suppressed a giggle at the way he tripped over himself to make sure what he meant was clear.

"That gratitude is going the wrong way, Hudson. You've been nothing but kind since you met me and it means a lot. I might not even be alive if it wasn't for you meeting up with us and taking me on. I certainly would have gone home if I'd been separated from Vaughn, not considering someone might be there waiting. Where would I be then?"

"Let's just say it's a good thing we don't have to find out," he said and there was a gravelly quality to his voice that caused it to travel over her and through her.

Anisa slowly exhaled the breath she'd been holding. The thought of this man staying over at her place sent a skitter of awareness over her skin. And she felt an ache that she hadn't experienced in far too long. Maybe ever.

"I'm ready to go whenever you are," she said. Maybe they could get answers at her apartment.

6

"You asked me about my relationship status a while ago," Anisa said when they were halfway to Austin. The first half of the ride had gone by in easy conversation. Hudson figured he hadn't said as many words if he'd added up his conversations from the entire past week. His throat should be dry and his jaw tired. They weren't.

"It's none of my business," he quickly said, not wanting to break up the flow they had going. Shock of all shocks, he *liked* talking to Anisa and he didn't want it to stop. He couldn't remember the last time he'd kept a conversation going this long without sex on the table.

"It's okay. I just wasn't ready to talk about it earlier," she explained.

He wasn't exactly sure what had changed but he'd felt the shift too. The easy way they had with each other was nice, especially considering how much the air charged with electricity anytime she was within arm's reach.

"You don't have to tell me anything now either," he said, not wanting her to feel obligated.

"My fiancé was killed in a boating accident. Neither of us knew about the pregnancy at the time," she said, her tone even-keeled. In fact, it was too level for the passionate person she was.

"Can I ask how far along you are?"

"Six months," she stated. This time, there was a hint of sadness in her tone.

"I'm sorry for your loss," he said and meant it. He couldn't imagine how horrible it must have been to lose someone she loved so out of the blue.

"Can I be honest?" she asked.

He figured the explanation for the steadiness in her tone when she talked about her fiancé was coming.

"Of course, you can," he said. "I don't know another way and I don't trust people who don't feel the same."

"I almost didn't keep the baby," she said. "I considered all my options, not the least of which was handing the little bean off to a deserving family."

"Bringing up a baby on your own is hard. No one can blame you for making sure you were up to the task. The worst thing a parent could do would be keep a child they couldn't handle or care for," he said.

"Believe it or not, I know I can bring up this child on my own or otherwise," she said. "Not that I don't have days where the prospect freaks me out big time. It has more to do with how I felt about having Kevin's baby."

"You're going to be an amazing mother. The kid is lucky to have you," he said without hesitation. Then added, "I don't know this Kevin person but he's crazy for making you question anything about having a relationship with him."

"How do you know?" she asked, sounding in true shock. "About the good mother part?"

"A few things. Every time you seem worried or scared, you cradle your stomach in a protective manner," he said.

"I do?" She sounded genuinely surprised and her reaction made him chuckle.

"Yes," he confirmed.

"Oh," she said. She paused a long moment before shaking her head like she was cleaning out the cobwebs. "Well, thank you."

"It's just my observation," he stated.

"I appreciate the confidence." She reached over and touched his forearm, causing all kinds of electricity to course through him. "It really means a lot."

"No problem." He kept his hand on the wheel and his gaze on the stretch of highway in front of them. Still, his chest swelled with pride that he could help her feel more confident in what had to be a scary situation to face alone.

She was quiet for a few moments.

"Kevin and I had broken up around New Year's," she continued. "And the reason was because he asked me to check something on his laptop and I stumbled onto a secret e-mail account that I was apparently not supposed to find. He'd been seeing someone else since the summer before. Someone he'd met on a guy's trip to Vegas. She was from Austin."

"I'm sorry to hear it. Being cheated on is the worst, and it breaks a trust that can never be recovered," he said, remembering the time it had happened to him. It had been during his last year of high school and had been worse than the mono he'd had freshman year. He didn't want to get out of bed for weeks on both counts.

"You would think. My ex was good though. It took three months, but he convinced me that he was sorry and he'd learned his lesson. He asked for a second chance. At first, I told him that he was crazy and I would never be able to take him back. He persisted and, honestly, seemed genuinely committed to our relationship," she said. "To be perfectly honest, I could admit to holding back. I had a history of being ready to walk at the first sign of trouble."

"Once you get burned, it's easy to slip into that pattern," he agreed. Had he done the same? If he was being honest, he could admit to getting bored easily. Was it something more? Was he ready to cut bait before a relationship could take root? Probably.

"I couldn't agree more," she said with a wistful smile. "Apparently, that's not the right attitude if you want to make it long-term."

"Probably not," he said. "He still shouldn't have cheated though."

"Nope," she stated. "And I should have learned my lesson the first time. But I let myself be convinced that moving in together would solve everything. I held out for a minute before I agreed to try. Then, he died before we got the keys to the place."

"I know I've already said it, but I truly am sorry." He couldn't imagine going through something like that after losing her brother. In fact, the loss of her family probably influenced her.

"When he died, *she* was in the boat with him," Anisa said, her voice was a mix of anger, raw edge, and bewilderment. "It's been six months now, he's gone, and I still can't seem to forgive him."

"That qualifies as a new level of impossible to process," he said, thinking she was one of the strongest people he'd ever met. "What made you decide to keep the baby, if I may ask?"

"His parents," she admitted. "I've gotten close to them

and they lost their only child. How could I take this bean away from them too?"

Anisa's heart knew no bounds. Hudson's respect for her grew the more he got to know her.

"They don't have a lot of money or they probably would have offered to bring up the baby on their own if I couldn't handle it," she said.

"Doing what you're doing is brave, Anisa." His admiration for her grew leaps and bounds too.

"You should have seen their eyes when I told them I was pregnant," she said and for the first time in this conversation her tone lightened. "The way they finally sparked for the first time since learning they'd lost Kevin."

"They sound like sweet people," he said. "No one should have to lose a child even when they're grown."

"It goes against the natural order of things," she said. Then, she turned the tables, "Do you ever think about having kids someday?"

"No," he admitted.

"Really?" she asked.

"Why does that news surprise you?" His curiosity was piqued.

"I don't know," she said on a shrug. "You come from such a big family. I just figured you might want the same for yourself at some point."

"My brothers have all recently found their life partners, and they seem happy," he said. "I just never really thought marriage and family was for me."

"Oh," she said. There was so much disappointment in that one word that it almost made him second guess whether it had been a good idea to express his opinion. Or was there something buried deep inside him that might want those things someday?

Either way, why did her opinion of him count so much? They barely knew each other and yet he couldn't deny that he didn't like the feeling of disappointing her.

"I'M a firm believer everyone has to make decisions that are right for them," Anisa said, trying to quash the disappointment in her tone at the revelation. She shouldn't care whether or not Hudson Firebrand ever planned to marry or have kids. So, why was did her chest suddenly deflate?

"As long as we're being honest, I've been considering leaving the ranch to break off and do my own thing for months now," he said.

"Sounds like a new adventure," she said, going with the flow on it and masking her surprise.

"I've been toying around with starting a taco business in Austin," he said.

"I would definitely be a regular if you could beat Torchy's," she quipped. "That does sound like a big leap though, from ranching to tacos."

"Yep," he seemed to agree wholeheartedly. "Part of the appeal is getting away from my big family. There's been too much discord since my grandfather passed away. I was starting to think Vaughn had it figured out. He ducked out after high school when the conflicts were lower level. They've become full-scale attacks at this point, and it's tearing the family apart."

"Is that the main reason you need to get out on your own?" she asked.

"It's a big factor," he said. "The other bigger part is that Firebrand Ranch doesn't feel like home to me any longer. Everyone on my side of the family is settling down and starting families of their own. Even my younger brother is married with a kid."

"You should definitely avoid drinking from the same well," she teased, feeling lighter after she'd talked about Kevin, like some of the weight she'd been carrying around lifted. There was something about sharing with Hudson that lightened the weight that had been a thick heavy blanket around her shoulders far too long now.

"Exactly what I was thinking," he shot back. "But seriously, what you're doing. It's amazing, Anisa. I hope you know that."

She could feel a red blush crawl up her neck toward her cheeks.

"You're too kind," she said, trying to shake off the compliment. Besides, he had no idea how many times she'd reconsidered and second-guessed her decision. No one would accuse her of being a saint. She could be selfish and scared at the same time. She'd learned to keep waking up, and keep pushing through with the hope life would magically work out. The belief had gotten her this far.

Traffic was picking up as they neared Austin. Horns honked. Cars whipped in between other vehicles.

"Have you thought about where in Austin you might like to start a business?" she asked, guiding the conversation back on course.

"I figured I'd search for a spot downtown," he said with a shrug.

"Have you thought about trying to start a food cart first to see if you like the business? Those permits are easier to get and there would be less start-up investment," she said.

"I'm open to all ideas right now," he stated. "I have yet to set up a family meeting to discuss the idea. I've been holding off waiting for my father to get stronger after his stroke."

"Oh, Hudson, I'm sorry. I've been blabbering about all my problems—"

"Don't do that," he interrupted. "Your personal situation is just as important as what's going on with my family."

"Is it bad with your father?" she asked.

"He's been making good progress," he said. "It's part of why I put my plans on hold. The family needs to figure out how we're going to handle business now that our father isn't the same as he used to be. He won't be able to take on all the stress of running a multi-million-dollar operation. Then, there's the guilt that comes with knowing all my brothers are home now. Finally. Just as I'm about to head off. Of course, having Vaughn back is another game-changer for me. But I don't exactly know what his plans are as of now."

"I wish he could communicate and at the very least tell us that he's all right," she said. "He's been on my mind but I didn't want to keep asking about him. I trust that you'll tell me what's going on with him the minute you hear something."

"Without a doubt," he promised.

"He's strong and he's amazing at what he does," she said, needing to say those words out loud to reassure herself as much as anything. For reasons she couldn't explain, she felt a bond with Vaughn. She might have saved his life but he'd saved hers in return. Going out camping alone while pregnant was probably not her smartest move. Thinking about T.J., missing her only family, had clouded her judgment. The reasoning of this possibly being the only year she could honor his request considering there would be a baby in the mix next year seemed logical at the time. Of course, her emotions had been in charge for weeks and they'd gotten away from her. There were other ways to honor his memory, safer approaches.

"I just wish we knew what he was up against," Hudson said.

"He purposely didn't give me a whole lot of context because he said the less I knew, the better," she admitted.

"Sounds like military speak," he said.

"I guess so. He thought they might let me go if I ended up caught and genuinely didn't know anything," she stated. But now, she figured it was wishful thinking on his part.

"As a recap, we know the person or persons after him have military-like skills," Hudson said. "And Vaughn was most likely doing someone a favor, which put him in the line of fire."

"Sums it up all right," she agreed.

"I can't help wondering if anyone else in the family has heard from him recently," Hudson said. "I realize that I'm the one he asked to have meet him and not his brothers—or even mine, for that matter. But he might have been in contact with his family. He must be aware of the fact his mother is in prison awaiting trial."

Anisa gasped.

"I mentioned my family has been torn apart, right?" he asked but it was more statement than question.

"You did," she admitted, but this was a very big detail to leave out.

"My aunt got greedy. She convinced my grandfather to change his will to include their side of the family. He'd originally left them out, which wasn't right in the first place. Still, Aunt Jackie tried to work on him. His lawyer caught on and made the most recent will easy to dispute because the Marshall had left out a very important person from his life. A person he'd kept hidden from us our entire lives. When that person sent her granddaughter with a copy of a will he'd given to her, Aunt Jackie attempted to kill them both so that her other side of the family could keep the mineral rights," he explained. "There's been tensions between both sides of the family for years but nothing like this has ever happened. The entire thing shocked everyone, including my uncle, from everything I've heard. Since then, getting everyone in the same room to hash out our problems has been impossible. Throw in my father's stroke and no one wants to push him in case it happens again."

"Understandable," she said, realizing her delusion that being rich would solve ninety-nine percent of her problems. "And how have you been during all this?"

"I've been keeping my head down and doing my work, trying to stay as far away from all of it as possible," he admitted on a sharp sigh.

"I hope you won't take this the wrong way but it sounds like the taco business might be a way to walk away from your family's problems, rather than stick around and solve them together," she said, hoping he wouldn't kick her out of the truck for speaking her mind. She tried to hide the fact her palms were sweating from nerves at being so honest. Hudson had a way about him that set her at ease and made her feel comfortable enough to speak to him so frankly and about topics that were normally off-limits to people she barely knew. And yet, she did know Hudson on a soul level. At least, she believed she did.

His lips compressed into a frown.

7

Hudson might not like hearing the words Anisa
had just spoken, but he appreciated her honesty.
They also struck a chord with him and he wasn't
immediately sure how he felt about any of it.

"It's something to think about," he finally said for lack of
something better. Ideas were percolating, and he was taking
heed of the possibility he was running away from troubles
rather than face them head-on.

"Hey, don't listen to me. I don't know what I'm talking
about half the time anyway," she said, back-peddling. From
the sound of her voice, he could tell she was worried she'd
offended him.

"Don't worry about it," he said. "You've given me something to chew on. I couldn't say one way or another right
now. I've just been focused on cashing out and getting away
from Lone Star Pass. I hadn't really given myself time to
consider why I needed to do it so badly."

"It sounds like your family has been through a whole lot
in a short time," she said with sympathy.

"There's been a whole lot of good happening too," he pointed out.

"There are always bright spots in every situation," she said. "I've learned that in some cases, I have to look a whole lot harder to find them though. And in others, it sometimes takes months or years before I see it when I'm looking back. It's there though."

She'd given him some food for thought. It probably didn't help matters that everyone on his side of the family was now engaged or married. He had to give it to his brothers. They seemed genuinely happy. Hudson just couldn't imagine it for himself. Not now. Not in a year. Not in five years. But all of his brothers had slipped into their own little worlds and the family didn't feel the same anymore.

Bingo. Hudson had just nailed a sticky point. He didn't care much for the fact everyone around him was changing. The family dynamic was changing. Life was changing and he felt like he was standing still in the same spot where he'd been for years.

"You're making me look at home with a different lens," he said to Anisa. No one had challenged his thinking or opened him up to new ideas in far too long. Then again, his dating life had been anemic of late. The whole scenario was understandable during calving season. Everything had to be set aside then. But this was late September and calves wouldn't be born for months. This was the time to get out and hit Austin for live music and to hook up with new people.

Honestly, since summer started, he'd been knocked off balance. Hudson might not have been close with his grandfather but the man had been at the helm of Firebrand Ranch Hudson's entire life. The person who was supposed to step up and fill the Marshall's shoes was Hudson's father.

He'd had a stroke. To say life was in chaos at the ranch was a whole lot like saying cheese came from milk.

"I hope I'm not overstepping my bounds," she said with an earnestness that he appreciated in a companion.

"To be honest, I like that you feel comfortable enough with me to tell me what's really on your mind," he said. He'd been on too many dates where the other person was afraid to speak up or challenge him, or too busy trying to be anything he wanted, so she could bag a Firebrand. His last name came with many benefits, which didn't mean there weren't an equal number of downsides. Not always being able to relax and have a real conversation with the opposite sex was definitely on the 'con' list.

Being with Anisa was refreshing. This was also not a date, he felt the need to remind himself. In fact, it was about the furthest thing from a romantic encounter, no matter how much his heart wanted to argue the two of them had a connection he hadn't felt in years. Maybe ever.

"Thanks for trusting me with everything you've been through in the past year," he said, wanting her to realize how special she was to him.

"We've both been through the wringer, even if for different reasons," she said with a small smile.

Was that the reason he felt an unbreakable bond with Anisa? They were two people bonded in loss? In pain? Ready to hang onto each other as a life raft while floating in the middle of the ocean in a raging storm?

"I'll take what you said under consideration," he replied, thinking that he needed to be one hundred percent certain he wasn't focused on starting a business for the wrong reasons.

His cell buzzed as he sat through a light for the third time in downtown traffic. He'd make it through on the next one.

"Do you mind checking for me?" he motioned toward his phone which was sitting in the cup holder on the console in between them.

Anisa picked up the cell phone and checked the screen.

"It's from Vaughn," she said, the excitement in her voice was palpable. "It's a thumbs-up emoji, so I'll take that to mean he's okay."

"That's a good sign." Relief washed over Hudson. He could almost see himself living at the ranch with his cousin home.

"Wait, there's more. He's typing," Anisa continued. Her smile brightened.

A horn honk caused Hudson to glance up and realize the light had changed to green and he was holding up the line. He gave a courtesy wave as he pressed the gas, waiting not so patiently for more word from Vaughn. At least his cousin was alive. There was one huge weight off Hudson's shoulders. He didn't let himself dwell on the possibility Vaughn wouldn't come out of this in one piece but the thought had been stalking the back of his mind. He'd been unable to shut it out completely.

"This part is cryptic," she said. "Keep package."

"Sounds like he might be worried someone could be hacking into his phone and monitoring his messages," he said. "A skilled tech person can hack into a phone easier than it should be. They could pinpoint someone's location and run up charges, since most phones are linked to credit cards now."

"Wouldn't Vaughn know how to block it, though?" she asked.

"Good question," he conceded. "You're probably right.

He would at the very least have some kind of encryption on his cell."

"I'd forgotten all about this until now, but he mentioned being out of the military for almost half a year now," she stated, staring at the screen as Hudson inched through traffic toward their destination.

"My cousin has been out of the service for six months and this is the first time he's reaching out to me?" Hudson didn't bother to hide his shock. This information changed things. He'd been racking his brain up to now trying to figure out what Vaughn could have done within days of being a civilian again. But six months? He could have done pretty much anything. Was that somehow tied to the favor he'd been doing?

Hudson couldn't begin to imagine what his cousin could have gotten himself into. A whole heap of questions mounted. Why wouldn't he contact the family when he left the military? And why hadn't he contacted Hudson before now?

More questions surfaced about his cousin and what he'd really been doing for the past half year. Hudson knew exactly where to start looking for answers. Would his call to his uncle even be welcomed after everything the family had been through in recent months?

Six months.

"My cousin was out of the military before our grandfather died," Hudson said, thinking out loud.

"It's late September now. When did you lose your grandfather?" Anisa asked.

"Early June," he supplied, his mind reeling. "He didn't come to pay his respects. He didn't even show up when his mother was arrested."

"Did he even know about what has been happening with your family?" she asked.

"I have no idea." Hudson couldn't wrap his mind around any of this.

~

"WHAT CAN I DO TO HELP?" Anisa asked, realizing Vaughn wasn't just a mystery man to her anymore, even if his own cousin didn't seem to have a handle on who he was or what he'd become.

"When I figure it out, I'll clue you in. Right now, I'm speechless," Hudson admitted, and she hated the shock and uncertainty in his voice.

"We don't have any additional information right now, so I'd hate to jump to conclusions," she said. Her mind had snapped to awful words like, *assassin* and *covert operations*. If Vaughn's actions were above board, wouldn't he tell his family that he'd been released from the service? Especially considering all the events that had been taking place at the ranch.

"My mind is going to some pretty awful places," Hudson finally said.

"Same here," she agreed.

"Knowing my cousin, I'd say there was no way Vaughn would be capable of the kinds of acts that are popping to mind," he continued. There was a numb quality to his voice now.

"I can't say that I know him personally, but after being around him for a short time it's nearly impossible for me to believe he could be doing anything on the wrong side of the law." She figured Hudson needed to hear those words coming from her. She had, after all, spent the most time around Vaughn recently between the two of them.

Hudson's gaze locked onto the rearview mirror. Anisa craned her neck to get a view of what he was staring at. A black truck jacked up on big wheels that looked made for off-roading was speeding up toward their bumper.

Anisa gasped as she braced for impact.

"Hold on tight." Hudson swerved, making a quick right turn down a side road as his cell buzzed again.

She checked the screen and suppressed another gasp.

"It's from Vaughn and the text says not to go home," she relayed. "What isn't clear is whether or not he means me or you."

"I'm guessing based on what just happened, he means both of us," Hudson stated, tightening his grip on the steering wheel until his knuckles turned white.

Off-Road made a comeback and was snaking its way toward them. The front bumper was taller than Hudson's truck, so it was impossible to get a visual on the driver through the windshield.

"Call 911 and tell the dispatcher you want to report a reckless driver," Hudson instructed.

Anisa did and gave specific instructions on cross streets as they moved through traffic. She held the phone down in her lap. "She is asking if I want to stay on the line."

"Might as well," he said. "That way you can shout out streets as we pass them."

"Okay," she said. "Good idea."

"Get down on the floorboard as fast as you can," Hudson instructed as he sank down in his seat.

Anisa unbuckled and flew down as the first shot was fired. She put the cell to her ear. "Did you hear that? He's shooting."

"Yes, ma'am," the young female voice responded. "Tell the driver of your vehicle to stay calm. My nearest officer is three minutes out."

Anisa relayed the message to Hudson.

"A lot can happen in three minutes," Hudson said on a sharp sigh as he cut the wheel left so fast and hard it felt like they came up on two tires for a half second. "If we were in Lone Star Pass, this would go a whole lot easier. Out here, I don't have my bearings and traffic is a nightmare. I'll try to get back to the highway, where I can open up the engine. This one has been souped up and we should be able to put some distance between us and the black truck."

"Sounds good to me. Tell me when I can reclaim my seat," she said, not loving being down on the floor where she couldn't see what was happening.

"I've lost him for the time being...well. No. He's coming back around," Hudson said. He honked his horn, then practically laid on it. "I sure hope these folks get off the sidewalk before I run them over."

It was a chilling thought and yet she knew he wouldn't hurt a single person on purpose.

One of the crazy things about living in downtown Austin was the fact there were always students around. University of Texas had around fifty thousand students, all of which seemed to mill around on the streets all day, every day, and nights too. Basically, the students were out twenty-four-seven in a sea of burnt orange t-shirts.

"Move. Move," Hudson said, honking the horn as another shot rang out.

Screams could be heard along with the sounds of tires squealing.

"Get out of the way," Hudson said through clenched teeth.

"How are we doing?" Anisa asked after saying another little protection prayer. She'd never been particularly religious but figured praying couldn't hurt. Besides, they needed a miracle based on the look on Hudson's face.

"We might have to get out and run," he stated as his gaze narrowed. He searched left to right and then studied the rearview for a few long seconds. "How are your legs feeling about now?"

"I can do whatever is necessary to get out of this alive and intact," she said. She wasn't kidding. She would do anything to keep her baby safe.

"There's a strip shopping center coming up on the left. I may be able to lose this guy long enough to let you sneak out of the truck and duck behind a car in the parking lot," he said.

"I don't want to break off from you," she said, feeling her pulse rise at the thought.

"It's not my favorite idea either, but I can distract them and you can get to safety," he explained. "We don't have a lot of time before I make the turnoff, so let me know what you want to do."

Anisa hesitated for a brief moment.

"We should stick together," she said but there was no certainty in her voice. They *should* split up. It made logical sense. But she feared she would never see Hudson again once the cops were involved. And where would that leave her in the long run?

Hiding out somewhere on her own? She didn't have the first idea how to survive the kind of person or persons who were after Vaughn. Then again, being pregnant probably slowed Hudson down. He could have parked and taken off running by now in the downtown traffic. Was she being selfish by wanting to stick together?

8

Hudson bit back a curse. There was not a world that existed in which he wanted to split up, but it might be the safest option for Anisa and the baby. All these quick turns that were jostling her around couldn't be good for the pregnancy. Or the stress for that matter. If she could duck into a restaurant or store until he could shake this guy or the law could catch up to them, maybe she could calm her nerves enough to hit the reset button.

He started to open his mouth to argue with her comment but the magic sounds of sirens cut through the air. Help wasn't far and that was the first big break they'd caught since the truck started targeting them. Glancing in the rearview, Hudson realized the Off-Road driver must've panicked.

"He just turned right," he said, rattling off the street name so Anisa could relay it to the dispatcher. This didn't seem like a good time to chide himself for not running his cell phone through Bluetooth into his truck so there wouldn't have to be all this back and forth through Anisa.

When he'd bought the pickup last year, he couldn't think of one good reason to set up the system. In Hudson's day-to-day life, cell phones weren't prominent.

"Is it safe for me to climb back in the seat?" Anisa asked after she relayed the information to dispatch.

"I believe so," he stated, giving her a hand up as he kept his left hand on the wheel. Be careful of glass from the window being shot. He maneuvered onto the side of the road with ease; multitasking had never been a problem for him. If Hudson was alone, he'd have no trouble following the jerk and seeing this through. Anger ripped through him at the thought he couldn't finish this right here and now after someone had threatened them and tried to run them off the road. There was precious cargo in his truck in Anisa and the baby, and he wanted to treat them both like fine bone china. "Do you mind telling the operator we're stopped in front of Fresh Beans Coffee?"

Anisa immediately spoke into the phone, passing along the information. Her voice lowered an octave when she was under duress. He thought about her job as an ER nurse and wondered if her calm-in-the-storm demeanor was a byproduct of her career field or if she'd been born that way. Either way, it was impressive.

"Yes, thank you," Anisa said. She looked at Hudson and locked gazes. "The off-roading truck made it onto the high-way. The police are giving chase, so hopefully they'll be able to nab the..." Her voice trailed off and she glanced down at her belly as though the little one might be able to hear her swear. She raised her eyes to meet his after being quiet a few more seconds. "Another officer will be here in a minute or two to take our statements."

"We should be safe here then." Hudson expanded the

GPS map to show the location of the highway and then pointed. "He must have entered here."

Anisa nodded.

"At least he's moving away from us and the police are on his tail," she said. "His vehicle is unmistakable, so it'll be hard to hide."

A chopper flew overhead. Anisa blinked up. "Looks like he's headed in the same direction. The cops will get him. There's no way he can escape in the Off-Road with this much heat on him."

"Are you okay?" he immediately asked after nodding. His thoughts were running along the same line.

"Me? Yes," she said with a quick glance down toward her stomach.

"And the baby?" he continued.

"So far, so good," she said with a sigh that sounded a whole lot like relief.

Hudson let out the breath he'd been holding. For reasons he couldn't explain and didn't want to examine, he cared deeply about what happened to this mother and child. Anisa was intelligent and caring. She deserved to have someone who looked after her despite the fact she could handle herself. He hadn't come across someone like her in a long time. Ever? Instinct told him that it wasn't likely he would meet someone like her in the future either. She didn't seem to realize how special she was, and it wasn't his place to tell her even though he felt an unexplained bond.

He reached out and took her left hand in his right. The connection set off fireworks in his chest. Ignoring them, he tightened his grip on her hand. She squeezed his in response.

"I see someone from law enforcement pulling up behind us," he said after scanning the rearview.

Anisa said a few *yes's* into the phone before nodding and moving her mouth away from the receiver. "This is Officer Pruitt. She will be taking our statement." Anisa thanked the dispatcher as Hudson opened his door. He greeted the five-feet-six-inch, auburn-haired officer before rounding the truck and opening Anisa's door for her.

The trio stood on the sidewalk in front of Fresh Beans Coffee as Officer Pruitt asked them to relay everything that had just happened. Hudson squeezed Anisa's hand. He needed to go out on a limb and hope she didn't tell the officer everything about their situation. Hudson had no idea if Vaughn was in trouble with the law and he didn't want to bring his name up if he didn't need to.

"Could I see both of your IDs?" the officer said after introductions.

"I don't have mine with me," Anisa said and there was a hint of panic in her voice. "I realized that I left my purse back at my boyfriend's ranch about halfway here. He has a key to my apartment so it's not a big deal but I didn't think I would need my purse. Plus, all these pregnancy hormones have made me forgetful. I'd swear I'd lose my head if it wasn't attached."

There was a warmth to Anisa when she spoke that seemed to resonate with the officer. She also had the ability to think on her feet. She'd come up with a cover story quickly and easily, keeping that calm head even now.

Hudson pulled his wallet out of his back pocket and handed over his ID. The officer held up a finger before excusing herself. She walked back to her vehicle and typed into the keyboard mounted on her dashboard. He figured she was running a check to see if he had any outstanding warrants while she had him there.

The officer returned a few minutes later, handing over

his license after thanking him for his patience. His last name seemed to resonate with her since she came back with a different demeanor than before. Now, she seemed to be intimidated by him. Or maybe curious was a better word.

"Tell me what happened in your own words," Officer Pruitt said to Anisa. The officer's voice had a calm and compassionate quality to it.

Hudson held his breath waiting for Anisa's response. They hadn't rehearsed what to say and he hoped she wouldn't give up too much information.

"My boyfriend was driving me home and this jerk in a big truck came roaring up behind us," Anisa began. Hudson slowly released his breath as she threw her hands up in the air. "He tried to ram our bumper for apparently no reason."

"Road rage," Hudson interjected. "It had to be. I've never seen anything like it but then that's the reason I live in the country." The sheer amount of traffic and people congestion had him wondering how long he would survive in a place like Austin. There was a definite vibe to the city, and a whole lot of folks crammed into a small space. Strange, he'd been here plenty of times in the past and wasn't too bothered by all the activity. Then again, he was looking at the place from a new lens now. One that said he might try to settle here and put down his own roots. The idea was losing steam.

"Did you get a look at the driver of the vehicle?" Officer Pruitt had a no-nonsense demeanor. Her hair swished around in the ponytail as she compressed her lips and frowned.

"I couldn't see a thing with those big tires," Anisa admitted.

Hudson confirmed the same thing with a nod and a sharp sigh. He wished that part wasn't true. It would have been nice to have a description of the person trying to kill him and Anisa. Her place was off limits now. In fact, he needed to get her out of Austin and away from here as fast as possible.

"What about plates on the black vehicle?" Officer Pruitt asked after they gave a description.

"I didn't see anything on the front," Anisa said.

"Neither did I," Hudson said. "But then I was busy driving and avoiding a bullet."

Officer Pruitt shook her head.

"You said your boyfriend here was driving you home," the officer said.

"Yes," Anisa stated. "I'd been at the ranch with him."

The word *boyfriend* sounded a little too right coming out of the officer's mouth and, surprisingly, his hand didn't automatically reach for his collar to loosen it at the thought. Instead, he wanted to lift up their linked fingers in a display to the world they were together. The urge shocked Hudson more than he cared to admit.

ANISA FINISHED GIVING her statement to the officer and leaned into Hudson as they waited for clearance. He'd looped his arm around her waist at one point during the interview with a wink to let Anisa know it was for show. They were supposed to be boyfriend and girlfriend, so he was just selling the idea. And yet her heart couldn't stop racing.

Why did her heart also protest at the word *selling*? This seemed like a good time to remind herself the two of them weren't in an *actual* relationship. She also couldn't explain why she felt so protective over Vaughn, except to say he'd kept her alive. There was clearly something going on with him and that something had to be big for all this attention they were getting. After talking it through with Hudson, questions were forming in her thoughts. In her heart of hearts, she didn't believe Vaughn was capable of breaking the law despite the circumstances. She had to admit it was strange that he hadn't been home considering he'd been out of the service for six months already.

Why would he avoid the ranch? His mother had been arrested for attempted murder. Wouldn't a son race home to be by her side? Vaughn didn't strike her as someone who didn't care about his family. In fact, he seemed to be doing his best to lead whoever was after him away from them.

There were so many questions when it came to Vaughn. Since everything had happened so fast after he'd reached out to them, she hadn't had a chance to respond to his text. The fact he'd sent a text and didn't call could indicate he was on the run. Was he sending a note as fast as he could before ducking out of cell range again?

They would reply to his messages. Would he respond?

Again, the question of what he could have possibly gotten himself into popped up. Again, no answer came to mind. All she could do at this point was scratch her head until they figured it out or he handled it and explained himself.

Standing this close to Hudson, his warm woodsy and musky scent filled her senses, sending warm sensations through her body in wave after wave. Her body hummed with electricity at every point of contact with his. She wrapped her arm around him, telling herself she was just participating in the rouse, but it was so much more than that. He was grounding her and keeping her sane in a world that had shifted into chaos around her for the past several days.

She bit back a bitter laugh. That world had been chaotic for far longer than just a few days if she took into account Kevin's accident, the cheating, T.J.'s death, and now little bean.

For the past year, Anisa had been head-down focusing on work to get through the day. The pregnancy had been a complete shock but had also forced her to put her shoulders back and think about living in the real world again.

A baby would need Anisa's full physical and mental faculties to be sharp and on point. A baby would force Anisa to look up again and think about her future after living in a thick, dark cloud. A baby would require Anisa to start thinking about finding a way to stop lingering in the past.

Babies were about the future and this one deserved at least one parent who was fully invested.

The past few months, once she'd done the math and realized how long it had been since she'd had a period, had been her taking small steps toward reclaiming a life. The second bedroom of the apartment she was supposed to share with Kevin would be turned into a nursery, rather than an office for him to work from home.

Life was about small shifts and figuring out how to navigate the changes that came with all the things she couldn't control.

Funny, she still hadn't unpacked all of her boxes or hung any pictures. Grief was a strange thing and so was the lack of ability to get closure. Because finding out that Kevin had still been continuing the affair meant the engagement would have been off.

Officer Pruitt climbed out of the driver's seat of her SUV and walked over with a frown.

"Everything okay, Officer?" Hudson immediately asked.

He seemed to instinctively pull Anisa closer against his body in a protective manner.

"With you two," Officer Pruitt started, "yes. Unfortunately, the driver of the vehicle escaped."

"How is that even possible?" Anisa asked, dumbstruck at the possibility. The vehicle was enormous and distinct.

"Austin traffic," the officer shrugged her shoulders but there was something she wasn't telling them based on the way she immediately glanced down at her black shoes then looked up again. "You guys are free to go." She pulled a card out of her front shirt pocket. "If you remember anything else, my number is on the card."

"Thank you," Hudson said, and she could hear the shock in his voice.

"Have a nice rest of your day," the officer said. It seemed like she couldn't get away from them fast enough.

"Mind if we stop in for coffee before we head out?" Hudson asked.

"Sure," Anisa answered, thinking she could use a decaf iced tea for the road. "Where to next?"

"My first thought was the ranch, but Vaughn's message warned us not to go home," he stated as he held the door open for her.

The coffee shop was lively with a line of students wearing burnt orange Hook 'em Horns t-shirts with various bottoms. They were in everything from boxer shorts to thick sweatpants despite the warm temperatures. Haircuts and lengths came in all shapes and sizes with long and straight being the go-to for most of the girls. Fresh-faced, they either stood in line with their eyes glued to their phone screens or were already seated and staring at their laptop screens.

At least the place had a calming effect on Anisa. This was a familiar Austin vibe. Although, she could see herself getting used to living at a place like Hudson's. Camping? Not so much. But his cabin had every modern luxury, with style to boot; it hardly felt as wild as the rugged outdoors that surrounded it.

Her mind really was bouncing around if she was thinking about the décor at Hudson's place. She needed to refocus. First question. "Should we try to respond to Vaughn's texts now?"

"I meant to do that," Hudson admitted as they took another step closer toward the order counter. He fished his cell from his pocket and fired off a text.

The doors opened and closed so much the temperature of the coffee shop was almost identical to the weather outside, a little too warm for her taste. Austin was known for being hot, which made for better falls and winters. She could do without all the rain in the spring and forget the pavement-melting summers. Still, Austin was her new home even though it didn't feel much like it without T.J.

Thinking about her brother caused her heart to ache. She'd kept herself so busy since his death that she hadn't given herself much of a chance to reflect on their times together. There'd been many. He'd had one of those devilish smiles that meant he was up to no good but his kind heart kept him from getting into real trouble. He liked breakfast tacos more than any one human should. He would often surprise her with them at the end of a long shift when she worked deep nights.

Hudson stood behind her, wrapping his arms around her. It was difficult to stay in a bad mood when she could feel his strong muscled chest against her back. She leaned into him, into his strength, not realizing until in that moment how much she needed someone who could prop her up. She just didn't let herself go there down the self-pity route. Missing her brother was an ache in her chest the pregnancy had somehow eased, and now being with Hudson was like salve to the broken parts inside her.

They inched a little closer to the counter.

"Thank you," she said to him, the low hum of conversation as folks waited nearby for their orders to be called drowned out her words so no one else could hear her.

"For what?" he seemed genuinely caught off guard by the comment.

"For everything. For being here with me and making sure I got home okay," she began.

"You didn't, though," he pointed out.

"No. But I would have if that jerk hadn't been anticipating our arrival," she defended.

He didn't comment so she could tell her response resonated.

"And the little things you're constantly doing to make me feel comfortable, comforted, and protected," she continued.

She could have sworn she felt his skin warm. Was he embarrassed?

"It's nothing," he tried to say but she reached for his hands and linked their fingers.

"Not to me, it isn't. It's everything," she continued. "You're the reason the baby and I are safe right now. And you made sure we were fed and have had plenty of hydration." She bit back a yawn, feeling the surge of adrenaline from the whole episode draining. "And now I can tell you're formulating a plan to keep us out of harm's way."

"You're important to me, Anisa," he said and his voice was low and gravelly. It managed to weave around her heart and squeeze. Other places were brought to life too but those weren't appropriate to think about in a public place. "I need to make sure you're protected until the threat is gone."

He pulled out his cell phone again and checked the screen.

"Still no word from Vaughn," he started, "and I have no idea how long this thing will last. But I do have a few ideas about how to tackle the problem and get some answers. We'll start with figuring out where Vaughn went when he left the military. I'm still confused as to where he's been. I need to call my uncle, but that phone call needs to take place in a private setting. I have no idea how it's going to go and I don't want everyone around hearing my family's problems."

He might have moved on with the conversation, guiding it back on track, but Anisa was still trying to figure out if she'd heard wrong. Had he just said she was important to him? Because her heart felt the same way about him and yet there was no way anything could work between them. She was a nurse tied into another six months in her lease. Not to mention the fact she was about to be a mother. Her life was in Austin. His was in Lone Star Pass. And the divide between the two places had never felt greater.

9

D rinks in hand, Hudson walked alongside Anisa to the truck, his thoughts spinning in a few different directions as he scanned the road to make sure it was safe. Thoughts of his family, and whether or not his uncle would give him the time of day, plagued him. Thoughts of his cousin and whether or not Vaughn was alive in a ditch somewhere struck him. And, finally, thoughts of Anisa and whether or not she felt the same electrical current running between them he did kept cycling through his mind.

Hudson didn't do one-night stands, and besides Anisa's life was here in Austin. This visit, being around all these people like he was in some twisted ant farm made him realize he'd gotten caught in the trap of the grass being greener. All the drama surrounding his family needed to be dealt with by sticking around the ranch. His conversation with Anisa had his wheels turning, wondering about his real motivation for the taco business.

At the truck, he surveyed the area to ensure no one seemed too interested in them or acted too casual. Both were indicators that they were being targeted again or at the very least watched. He was still trying to figure out how Off-Road managed to flee the law. The officer's explanation, or lack thereof, had him all kinds of concerned. Why had she been so ready to make her exit after delivering the news?

The whole scenario had his radar up.

"Where to now?" Anisa asked once they had on their seatbelts.

Hudson started the engine of the truck and pulled out of the parking spot. Someone honked. He waved but the only way to get around in Austin traffic was to be forceful. Try applying the same courtesy rules as he observed in Lone Star Pass, and he'd be eaten alive. So, he wasn't sorry he'd made his move. It was that or sit there in that spot forever. Drivers in Austin had forgotten two words, yield and courtesy.

"Since we haven't heard back from Vaughn and it doesn't seem safe to stay in my truck now that we've been identified, I thought we'd stop off a car rental place and change vehicles first. Then, grab a room nearby so we can figure out our next move," he said, figuring they needed a few minutes to regroup and come up with a plan.

"Okay," Anisa said. There was a distant quality to her voice now. One that had him worried she might be checking out on him. It was the way some folks dealt with stress. Being a trauma nurse, she must have developed quite a talent for tucking away her feelings so she could get through a shift.

Like a volcano biding its time, waiting for a tipping point, stuffing emotions down deep would eventually end in total destruction.

"Tell me what you're thinking," he said, trying a nudge to see if he could get her talking.

"Nothing," she said before issuing a sharp sigh. "Everything."

"Start with the first thing that comes to mind," he urged. It occurred to him the family had the same problem. Always stuffing down emotions and never talking about anything important. Everyone processed events in their own separate way and there was never a discussion about a problem. If it involved the business, solutions were decreed by the Marshall so it wasn't like anyone had a say in the first place. Was that the reason everyone had gotten so good at stuffing down their feelings? Speaking would have been a lost cause anyway?

"I can't," she said. "There's too much."

Hudson navigated onto a side street and, miracle of all miracles, found a place to park. He kept the engine running as he excused himself for a second to send a text to his older brother Adam requesting a room and vehicle be arranged under someone else's name near Austin pronto, preferably not under the Firebrand name. Adam's response was immediate, and before Hudson could revisit his conversation with Anisa, information started rolling in.

He plugged in the name of the bed and breakfast into GPS and learned Adam had rented the place out. Security would be sent to keep watch, so whatever was going on, Hudson and Anisa should be safe.

The car rental place was four blocks from Hudson's current location. The city had one thing on small-town living, convenience. It seemed like everything a person could want was practically within spitting distance.

Hudson briefed Anisa on the details. She opened her mouth to speak and then clamped her mouth shut as he navigated through the one-way streets to the car rental place.

"What were you going to say?" he asked.

"Promise you won't get offended?" she asked and there was a pensive quality to her voice.

"I'll do my best. No guarantees," he said with a half-smile as he tried to lighten the mood.

"What kind of money does your family have, that these things can be arranged with a text? I've heard of the Firebrands in name but that's about all I know." She sounded stunned. "And how are you so grounded? Vaughn was the same way and it doesn't make any sense to me."

Hudson was so used to this life, it rarely ever occurred to him how it must look to a stranger.

"Well, I've lived this way my entire life so it's second nature to me. But, there's rarely ever an occasion where we need to make things happen on a dime. No matter how much money we have, we don't take it lightly. To my brothers and I, at least, money is nothing more than zeroes in a bank account. It's what you do with your life that matters," he said, and he could hear the defensiveness in his own voice. "I don't mean to get on a high horse here. We appreciate everything we have and don't take it for granted. Each of us has had our own battle with having so much handed to us. It's important for each of us to make our own way and carve out our own destiny."

He pulled into the car rental parking lot as he finished his sentence.

"I'm sorry, Hudson," Anisa said as she reached over and touched his forearm. "I didn't mean to step on any toes. Going without money for so long, it's easy to fall into the trap of thinking it can solve everything. It's a limited view and I apologize if I'm being offensive. You and your cousin are two of the most grounded people I've ever met and that's saying a lot because in my line of work I come across literally every type of person imaginable. You guys are the real deal and deserve every good thing you have."

"Everyone deserves food on the table and a roof over their heads," he stated. "Working the land, being connected to something bigger than yourself is probably the best way to keep your boots rooted in reality."

"You're smart and kind," Anisa said. He glanced over in time to see a red blush crawl up her neck at giving the compliments.

All he could do was shake his head and smile.

"You don't have to say all those things to smooth things over," he said, thinking about all the homeless folks they'd passed while driving downtown. "I'm not mad. Being worthy of everything we've been handed has been a lifelong battle. It's hit some of us harder than others. The more I stayed inside my head and in my little world, the more I thought about it. Being out here and seeing the way folks live and how some do without puts life in perspective. It's good to get those reminders."

"That's exactly what I'm talking about," Anisa said. "And I wasn't just being kind when I said those things. You *are* the real-deal, Hudson. I just haven't met anyone else like you and it's catching me off guard sometimes. I promise not to look at your life in one dimension any longer. There's so much more than what's on the surface, and it's one fine surface."

The last words brought the red blush back. So, Hudson did the only thing he could. He leaned over the console and kissed her.

∼

A LIVE WIRE seemed to break loose inside Anisa's body the

second Hudson came over the console. His thick lips were surprisingly tender, a contrast to the roughness of the days-old stubble on his chin. Together, they caused electrical impulses rocketing inside her, seeking an outlet and finding none.

Her entire body was alive with impulse as she urged him on, deepening the kiss. She parted her lips for him and he teased his tongue inside her mouth in a glorious kiss. He brought his hand around to cup her cheek, the roughness of his hands reminded her that he worked outdoors. She could only imagine what those fingers would feel like on her body.

When he pulled back, he surveyed the area, reminding her of the danger they could be in.

"I've been wanting to do that longer than I care to admit," he said, his voice low and husky. More of those sensitized shivers skittered across her skin. Her arms goosebumped. All she could think was how she wanted more of Hudson. An ache formed in her chest as he leaned back into the driver's seat, taking all his woodsy warmth with him in the move.

"I have too," she said low and under her breath. It probably wasn't a good idea to let her attraction to this man get out of control. Between her near-death experiences, the danger she was in, and her grief for her missing brother, her emotions were all over the place. "It was a great kiss."

She needed to leave it at that.

"I'm guessing by the sound of your voice that means you don't want a repeat," he said with so much disappointment in his voice she almost didn't speak her mind.

"It's not a good idea." She would leave it at that.

Anisa wasn't sure if she should be grateful or disappointed Hudson seemed content to leave the conversation on that note. He exited the driver's seat before coming around to her side of the vehicle. He opened the door for her. His lips compressed into a frown and he looked like he was holding something back.

This wasn't the right time to ask what was on his mind. They needed to grab the rental vehicle and then get to their next stop. The muffin she'd eaten from the coffee shop was barely holding her over, and she needed to eat a real meal soon.

Hudson linked their fingers as they walked into the lobby area. The man behind the counter immediately came around to greet him. He was almost a foot shorter than Hudson with brown hair in a side part with a short cut. His brown eyes were bright, and he had a slight frame with a broad smile and buck teeth. He reminded her of Howdy Doody minus the red hair and freckles as he be-bopped over to them. His nametag read, Artie.

"I have keys for you right here." Artie held out his hand, palm flat.

Hudson thanked Artie before taking the offering. Anisa took note of the fact Hudson didn't introduce himself.

"You'll be in the black BMW sport utility parked out front," Artie said practically beaming.

"Much appreciated," Hudson said before shaking Artie's hand.

"Thank you for doing business with us, sir," Artie said before flashing his smile at Anisa.

She was so used to exchanging greetings and introducing herself that she could admit to being thrown off by the exchange. Hudson smiled at Artie before reaching for Anisa's hand as they parted company.

The BMW had blacked-out windows and enough room for Hudson to be comfortable. After opening her door for her, he relocated a few things from his truck before claiming the driver's seat.

The little bean was active today and that made Anisa smile. She'd also noticed the kiddo seemed to perk up whenever Hudson spoke. Was it possible the baby could feel Anisa relax and was responding to its mother?

Mother. Anisa was still getting used to that term. She hadn't planned on being pregnant at twenty-seven years old. In fact, she'd been told getting pregnant would be difficult for her since she'd been diagnosed with endometriosis three years ago. Other than a little moment about the possibility of never having a family, Anisa hadn't been too upset about the diagnosis. In fact, it took the pressure off in some ways. She didn't have to worry about deciding to have a kid. Growing up with a father who'd ditched Anisa early in her life and a mother who couldn't wait to do the same, Anisa had decided it was probably not best to continue that genetic lineup.

Now that she was hitting the third trimester, she was beginning to believe she could do this. She could take care of this baby and not completely mess up the job in the process. The kiddo deserved at least one amazing parent.

Anisa couldn't help but think Hudson would make an amazing dad. Her kid deserved someone like him to look up to and look after it.

"If we end up staying the night here, I'd like to stay in the same room if that's okay with you," Hudson stated, breaking into her thoughts. She'd been so lost in her own head that she hadn't realized he'd pulled into the Bed and Breakfast where they were planning to set up basecamp.

"Okay," she said as her stomach picked that moment to grumble. "It's strange to think we're in my city and not staying at my apartment."

"You must be starving," he said, checking the clock.

"The muffin held me over, but I could eat," she said, thinking that statement should cover an entire pizza. Her stomach growled again, and the baby kicked.

"What was that?" Hudson asked.

She looked at him with a blank stare. "Not sure what you mean."

"That," he motioned toward her stomach as the baby started practicing for a soccer career. "Your shirt is moving."

"This little bean likes to go jogging around this time every day," she said, cradling her bump as he pulled into a parking spot and then turned the engine off.

"That's amazing." His eyes lit up and her heart took a severe hit.

"You can touch it if you want," she said. "Though I can't promise this one won't go for a field goal while you're at it."

"Can I?" he asked and then added, "What I mean is, should I? Is it okay to touch?"

His caution was endearing.

"Of course," she said. "There's quite a bit of protection around this little one."

"Boy or girl?" he asked.

"We'll both know when I give birth," she quipped. And then corrected the statement, "I'm not saying *you* would be at the birth because why would you? We'll figure out what's happening with your cousin and the bad guys will end up arrested long before this kiddo comes into the world. End of story. There will be no need for us to know each other any longer, and plus with our schedules and your lack of cell coverage on the ranch, we would never get the chance to talk to each other anyway." Well, hadn't she started puking out words?

Anisa put a hand up to stop Hudson from pitying her or

saying whatever it was that made his eyebrows pinch together.

"It was just a saying," she corrected. "I didn't mean anything by it."

"Too bad," he said low and under his breath. So low, in fact, she couldn't be certain it wasn't her imagination.

10

Hudson let Anisa place his hand on top of her small bump. He felt a thump and, much to his surprise, warmth spread through him like he'd never experienced. The child didn't belong to him and yet he couldn't deny a connection in that moment.

"Hey, little one. Be nice to your mama when you see her. She deserves to be treated like a queen after what she's been through and she needs you to be good to her," he said in a whisper.

The kiddo kicked in response.

"Did you feel that?" he asked Anisa.

She nodded and a smile brightened her hazel eyes. Not a moment later, she turned toward the passenger side window. For the life of him, Hudson couldn't figure out what he'd done wrong. The atmosphere in the SUV changed, though, and all he could feel was ice.

Rather than push her to speak when she seemed to need quiet, he exited the vehicle as security came out the front door of the B&B. The two-story could best be described as farmhouse quaint. It looked like something out of one of those home makeover shows, complete with half a dozen rockers scattered around a wrap-around porch. The white farmhouse had black shutters and flower boxes on the windows. There were plants hanging everywhere. The place looked like it required quite a bit of watering and upkeep. It had a homey quality to it and plenty of privacy since it was set off the road a bit.

He nodded toward the security guard, who was dressed in khakis and a black t-shirt, complete with mirrored sunglasses and a Stetson, before opening Anisa's door. He'd made a guess as to her clothing sizes so there would be clean clothes waiting once she got inside. He had no idea how long they were going to be staying and wanted to make her as comfortable as possible during their time here.

Stetson approached with his hand extended.

"My name is Paul Watson, sir. Pleasure to meet you face-to-face," Paul said. Hudson shook the outstretched hand in front of him.

"This is Anisa, and you already know my name," Hudson said to Paul, who tipped his hat in her direction.

Hudson reached for Anisa's hand and then linked their fingers.

"My girlfriend is hungry. Is the food ready?" Hudson asked. The muscles in Anisa's hand flinched ever so slightly. He hoped he hadn't overstepped any bounds by referencing her as his girlfriend. It was easier than explaining what he was doing with a pregnant friend.

"Yes, sir. Right this way," Paul responded, motioning toward the house. "The inside has been cleared and there's a secured phone waiting on the kitchen table just in case. The contact information for your brothers and other family members have been stored in it."

"Thank you," Hudson said to Paul as he did a visual

sweep of the surrounding area. Paul was from a top-notch security firm the family used from time to time.

"Yes, sir," Paul responded. It was clear from his age, demeanor, and haircut that he was recent military.

Hudson walked with Anisa onto the porch and then inside the home. The smells from the kitchen hit full force when they entered the foyer. It was then Hudson realized how hungry he was. When his mind was spinning, like when he was tracking poachers, he could go for days on nothing more than power bars. He needed to remind himself a pregnant person wouldn't be able to go so long. Anisa hadn't complained about being hungry. In fact, she hadn't complained about much of anything. But her stomach had done the talking and it said she needed food as soon as humanly possible.

"Do you smell that?" she asked, with the kind of enthusiasm he imagined he would hear from a kid who'd been unleashed inside a toy store.

"Waffles?" he asked, smiling.

"Heaven is more like it," she said as she made a beeline toward the smells. He did his best to keep up.

It wasn't difficult to find the kitchen, where two of his favorite things could be found, waffles and coffee. Both were fresh, hot, and ready to go.

"The owner cooked this up right before she was escorted off property for her own safety," Paul said, stopping in the hallway. "There are two guards on property in addition to me. We'll rotate every two hours, so you'll get to meet the others if you're here for any length of time. There's a shift change every twelve hours and we rotate that as well."

"This is great. Well done," Hudson said as he fixed a plate behind Anisa. On a butcher block island, there were all the fixings he could want. Fresh blueberries, several grades of maple syrup, powdered sugar, and what looked like homemade whipped cream along with freshly whipped butter.

"Thank you, sir," Paul said before adding, "I'll be within earshot if you need anything else."

Hudson nodded, which seemed to be the only signal Paul needed to leave them alone. After setting his plate down on the table, he fixed a cup of coffee.

"What can I get you to drink?" he asked Anisa.

"Is there milk?" she asked.

He checked the fridge, found a gallon, and then located a glass. He brought the offering to the table and then set it down in front of her. As she polished off her first waffle, he picked up the phone in the middle of the table and called Adam.

"Give me the rundown," Adam said after a quick hello.

"First of all, Adam, I have someone with me. Her name is Anisa and she's a nurse. She found Vaughn on ranch property and in pretty bad shape. She fixed him up and kept him alive long enough for him to hand her off to me," Hudson recapped. "She's here and you're on speaker. Okay?"

"All good here. Nice to meet you, Anisa," Adam stated.

"Same to you, Adam," she said in between bites.

"We haven't eaten, and I didn't want to wait another second before I called you, so excuse the chewing sounds," Hudson said.

"No problem," came the response. Adam's little girl made gurgling noises in the background and they were the cutest sounds. Hudson hadn't paid that much attention to them before but suddenly anything to do with a little baby interested him. "What is going on with Vaughn?"

"Did you know he's been out of the military for six months already?" Hudson asked his brother.

"Really? No, I had no idea," Adam stated. "He hasn't been on ranch property or Steven would have mentioned it."

"Steven Paine is head of ranch security," Hudson whispered to Anisa. She nodded as she finished another bite of waffle. It was good to see her get food inside her and enjoy it so much in the process. He turned his full attention to the call. "Which doesn't mean he hasn't been in contact with one of our cousins or our uncle."

"Do you think he would contact Aunt Jackie or go to a visitation where she's being held?" Adam asked.

"I highly doubt it, but there would be a visitor record on file if he did," Hudson pointed out.

"I'll see if we know anyone at the women's prison," Adam said. The thought of their Aunt Jackie being locked up for the rest of her life was a hard pill to swallow. Granted, she'd twisted off and gone to an extreme. She was getting what she deserved, being locked up and kept away from society. His heart went out to his cousins and uncle, though.

"That would be a great help," Hudson said on a sigh, thinking he didn't want to make the call he knew he had to. "I'll check in with Uncle Keif when we get off the phone."

"Okay," Adam said. "Are you sure about that?"

"No. Frankly, I don't want to, but it's necessary," Hudson stated. "I'd also like to see if anyone from Vaughn's unit knows where he went after being discharged." He paused as another idea popped. "Don't we have someone who can track down credit card usage? If we can follow his trail, we might be able to piece together where he was and what he was doing. Anisa mentioned he was doing someone a favor."

"It's possible but highly unlikely we can track him from credit card usage. Our accounts have extra security," Adam stated.

Right, Hudson should have remembered that.

"Anisa, did Vaughn mention anything about what was going on at home?" Adam continued.

"There wasn't much time for talking, to be honest," Anisa responded. "Even if there was, I wouldn't have quizzed him about his personal life. In fact, I was planning to get as far away from him as possible the minute I could. No disrespect intended."

"Understandable under the circumstances," Adam said. "We owe you for keeping our cousin alive. I hope you'll allow us an opportunity to thank you personally. The whole family is in your debt."

Hudson couldn't agree more on both fronts and yet he was still disappointed at the dead end.

"No thanks needed. I took an oath, and I take that seriously. I was just doing what anyone else would have done if they'd found him first," Anisa said.

She was wrong. A whole lot of people would have passed right on by that day, leaving Vaughn alone and vulnerable. He might not be here today if she didn't stumble upon him in the first place.

"We have a place to start right here in the family," Adam interjected.

"True. I'll let you know if I get anything from Uncle Keif," Hudson responded.

"Something will turn up with all of us on this," Adam said before adding, "I told the others about what was going on since we all work the land and someone could come across one of the folks after Vaughn. As for our cousins, I had Steven put out a warning that trespassers have been sighted and they are to be considered armed and dangerous."

"Makes sense to keep everyone on alert. I'll be sure to

explain the situation to Uncle Keif and ask him to funnel the information down as he sees fit," Hudson said before they exchanged goodbyes and he ended the call.

He took a couple of bites to get enough food in him to keep his stomach from growling while he made the next call.

The phone rang twice. One more and it would go into voicemail. For a split second, Hudson worried his uncle had checked the screen and decided not to take the call. Hudson used his personal cell for family calls so they would know it was him. Then, the ringing stopped, and Uncle Keif's voice came on the line.

"What can I do for you?" was all he said. Did he even know it was his nephew on the line?

"Uncle Keif, this is Hudson," he began.

"Yeah? What do you want?" His uncle's voice was direct and his tone was clipped, which was nothing new from the man.

"I have a question as to whether or not you've heard from Vaughn recently." Hudson figured he might as well dive right in.

There was a long pause.

"Why do you ask?" Uncle Keif asked.

Interesting. Wouldn't his uncle just give a response if the answer was *no*? First the pause, then the question.

"He reached out to me and asked me to keep watch over a package for him. Now, he's stopped returning my messages. I need to let him know that I have the package and I need to know when it's safe to return it," he said, giving as much information as he reasonably could. They both knew more than they were owning up to.

"How about this. If I see him or hear from him, I'll pass along the message," Uncle Keif said.

"That could work," Hudson said, thinking it was a baby step toward cooperation. He needed more, so he was going to have to give more. "Here's the thing. I think he's in some kind of trouble and I want to help. You know how close the two of us were growing up, so I was surprised when I learned he's been out of the military half a year already."

"How long did you say?" Uncle Keif asked. The man seemed unwilling to budge. Should Hudson cut bait and move on?

"About six months, the best I can tell. I just heard from him yesterday though," Hudson admitted. He'd given his uncle enough information without getting anything in return. "Sorry to have bothered you. I'm sure he'll get in touch when he can."

Before Hudson could end the call, his uncle muttered a curse.

"Hold on a second," Uncle Keif said. Did that mean he was willing to shed some light on Vaughn's whereabouts? Did Uncle Keif know where his son had been since leaving the service? Another thought struck. Did Vaughn get into trouble doing a favor for his father?

ANISA PERKED up as she listened to Hudson's conversation. He had the phone to his ear on this call so all she could hear were his responses. It didn't sound like he was getting very far just before he was about to hang up.

She sat a little straighter, slowly chewing the bite of waffle in her mouth as she watched Hudson pace back and forth in front of the sink. His eyebrows drew together as he said a few uh-huhs into the phone. After more pacing and cryptic responses, he thanked his uncle and ended the call.

"He knew, didn't he?" she asked.

"My uncle says he did know but that's about the extent of it," Hudson stated. "He said he found out when he tried to reach Vaughn after the Marshall's accident. Then, he went on a hunt for his son."

"Which ended with the two of them in contact?" she asked, but it was a rhetorical question.

"According to Uncle Keif, Vaughn reached out to him and said some of his friends got in touch with him to tell him that his father was looking for him," Hudson stated.

"Sounds peculiar, don't you think?" she asked. "Vaughn gets out of the military to—what?—immediately do a favor for someone? The Off-Road person from earlier sure seemed to have access to things us normal people don't." A thought struck her suddenly. "Wait, would it be possible that the helicopter might not have been Austin PD after all? It's possible Off-Road summoned it and that was how he managed an escape."

"Those are good points, but they don't explain why Vaughn would be on foot if he was doing some covert operation for the military, which it sounds like you're suggesting," he countered.

She nodded.

"So, the favor had to be someone on the outside. What about a member of his unit who got out before he did?" she said. "Could he have been protecting someone's spouse or carrying out a mission?"

"Everything is on the table at this point," he confirmed.

She nodded, then clamped her mouth shut. This situation was a real head scratcher.

"Let's check the news and see if there's anything about a police chase or a vehicle being abandoned on or near the highway," Hudson said. He held his cell flat on his palm as he walked over to the table and took a seat next to her.

Being this close, her body reacted, humming with need. Once again, she reminded herself that her hands were full with a pregnancy and a full-time job. One she would be getting back to in two days if she got the green light to return to work. Otherwise, she was going to have to take medical leave or call in sick. It was a sobering thought people who had the kind of power to summon a helicopter to evade the police had her personal information.

Potentially, she corrected.

Then again, the fact they were in Austin waiting for her meant they most likely had found her backpack. They were most likely waiting for Vaughn. Right? That would make the most sense. Although, they might try to use her to draw him out. Was it possible he had something of theirs?

"Now, I'm wondering if your cousin has some information these people need." She was thinking out loud.

"It could be information, or he might have proof they've done something wrong," he said, continuing the brainstorming.

"No good deed goes unpunished," she repeated. "Doesn't necessarily mean it's a favor. Maybe he was just stepping in for a friend and got caught up in something serious."

"At this point, all the scenarios we've brought up so far are possible," he said. "I just wish we had more clues to go on so we could narrow down the options."

"Did he say anything to your uncle that might help?" she continued.

"Nothing stood out," he confided.

"What if he's working for some blackwater-type agency and government officials are involved?" she asked.

"Then, my cousin is in even more trouble than we originally thought," he said, which was saying a lot.

She'd already tied Vaughn to covert work outside the military. Everyone knew these types of organizations existed, and she would bet money on the fact they were responsible for getting things done that couldn't go through proper channels. The country's freedom depended largely on these agents who did 'the dirty work.' Basically, they handled assignments off the books, so there would be no government approval necessary. These men and women operated like the CIA but were privately funded. She had no doubt those agencies would pull heavily from ex-military.

"Whatever Vaughn did as a good deed ended up putting him in the line of fire," she stated. "It could have been a favor or he could have been stepping in for someone." She paused. "We keep going round and round in circles on this subject, don't we?"

"There's just not enough information to do anything else. Plus, maybe you'll remember something else from your time with my cousin. I have very little to go on with my interaction with him. You were there to see it. All he did was hand you over and ask me to keep you safe," he said.

"Is it strange that he didn't tell us not to go home at the time?" she asked.

"Possibly," he stated.

"Do you think he realizes they have my backpack?" she asked.

"Anything is possible at this point," he confirmed. His cell buzzed in his hand. He checked the screen. "Unknown caller."

The two of them locked eyes for a long moment before he answered, and immediately put the call on speaker.

"Hello?" he said and she realized not giving his name

was probably on purpose. There was no reason to give the caller information they might not have.

"Hudson Firebrand?" a male voice came through, deep and sharp.

"Depends on who is asking," Hudson shot back with a weary glance toward Anisa.

11

"This is an associate of Vaughn Firebrand."

Questions popped into Hudson's mind, like where did this so-called associate get this number, considering it was a new burner phone? Was this man after Vaughn or did he truly know him? Hudson didn't trust this person as far as he could throw 'em. He wasn't giving the guy anything without getting something from them first to prove they were acquainted with Vaughn.

"Prove it," he said, acting like he couldn't care less one way or another. Sounding desperate wouldn't help their case. He had no plans to tip his hand.

"Vaughn's date of birth is—"

"Tell me something you can't get off a computer search as a skilled hacker," Hudson cut in. He didn't plan on wasting his time and figured he needed to get off the line so this call couldn't be traced if that was the play here.

"His grandfather recently died," the man said.

"Who is this?" Hudson asked.

"It's probably better if I don't say," he said.

"Then, I'm hanging up," Hudson moved his finger over the red 'end call' button and let it hover.

When no argument came, he pressed it. If that was a bluff, he'd just called it. The cell rang almost immediately. Hudson waited a couple of rings before answering. He didn't speak when he finally hit the green button to accept the call. Instead, he listened.

A chuckle came through the line, which confused Hudson to no end.

"I served with Vaughny, and he said you were a stiff son-of-a-gun," the same male voice from a few seconds ago came across the line. "He never mentioned how stubborn you are."

Hudson didn't respond.

"He must be in a whole lot of trouble for you to be this cautious," the guy said on a sharp sigh. "I heard his family has been poking around in his personal affairs recently. What can I do to help?"

"You still haven't identified yourself," Hudson stated for the record.

"It's best if we keep it that way," the guy said. He had the stiff, formal military voice that was so much like Vaughn's. "Suffice it to say I used to go by Hawk, and not because of any facial features. Let's just say I was good at finding things on the ground from the air when needed."

"Well, Hawk, I have no idea what's going on with my cousin and that's part of the problem," Hudson stated, figuring he wasn't exactly giving away the farm with his honesty.

"Tell me what you know so far," Hawk said.

"Not so fast," Hudson said. "I still haven't decided if I can trust you." Not that he had a whole lot to share or much of a choice.

"Let's see. Most of what I know about Vaughn comes from serving in the military and he purposely didn't have contact with his family during his service. Said he didn't like mixing up the two worlds and that he'd gone into the service to get away from 'the crazy' while his grandfather was alive," Hawk said.

Hudson had to admit, Hawk was pretty dead on. Those were the exact words Vaughn had used with Hudson when he'd asked Vaughn why he needed to leave so fast after high school graduation.

"He was also angry the fighting didn't seem to get any better over time," Hawk supplied.

"How did he know?" Hudson was curious, considering he'd been the closest to Vaughn and hadn't heard from his cousin once since leaving.

"He kept tabs," Hawk stated. "Did you know about Katy?"

"Roberts?" Hudson asked.

"That's the one," Hawk said.

"Why? Did he still talk about his high school girlfriend? He told me that he never wanted to speak to her again after her reaction to him going into the service," he said.

"Well, they stayed in touch," Hawk supplied. "She apparently wrote him a letter that he got the minute he got out of basic. Said she was being a selfish idiot and that she was proud of him for serving his country."

"Really? Interesting," Hudson noted. "I lost track of her after she headed north to Waco to attend Baylor University."

"The letters came for the first year and then they stopped," Hawk said. "Vaughny nursed a broken heart for the longest over that one. He dated a few others but the comparisons always came back to Katy. She would pop back into his life here and there but he kept his cards close to his chest when it came to her."

Hudson shouldn't be surprised and yet it was strange talking to someone who knew Vaughn better than his own family.

"I'm guessing she got tired of waiting for him or hooked up with someone else at a campus party, and decided to move on," Hudson said.

"Vaughny never said, and we all knew the subject was off limits," Hawk said. "So, have I proven myself worthy yet?"

"You know more about my cousin than I do," Hudson admitted, and the two had been best friends since birth, according to Hudson's mother.

"Where did you see him last?" Hawk asked.

"How do you know I did?" Hudson was a decent poker player. How could Hawk have read him so easily?

"Your hesitation gave you away," he informed. "If you hadn't seen or heard from him, you would have told me to kiss your backside before hanging up."

"Where did he go after he was discharged?" Hudson asked, turning the tables, intentionally skipping an answer. He wasn't quite ready to involve Anisa in this.

"My guess is that he headed where he always talked about going," Hawk said. "Back to the ranch."

"No one has seen him there, except for me and that was yesterday," Hudson stated.

"Interesting," Hawk said in a noncommittal tone. "The ranch was all he ever talked about."

"Did he say whether or not he planned to come back to work there?" Hudson asked out of curiosity more than anything else.

"All the time," Hawk said.

The line was quiet for a few beats.

"Vaughn said, 'No good deed goes unpunished,'" Hudson said, tossing it out there. "Does it mean something different to you than it does to me?" He figured he might as well throw that out there and see if it stuck.

"Not that I can think of," Hawk said. "To be truthful, my first thought is that he was going to track Katy down. He held onto her letters over the years, letters that came in fits and spurts. I think part of him believed he could show up and win her back."

"Maybe he got sidetracked along the way," Hudson said.

"If he did a favor for someone..." Hawk got quiet. "I can make a few calls and see if I can track down any information on who he might have been in contact with after being discharged."

"Fill me in on anything you get?" Hudson asked.

"From here on out, we're a team," Hawk stated with the kind of conviction that said he would back it up with action.

"I appreciate it and will reciprocate," Hudson stated, thinking this was probably the time to let him know about Anisa if they were truly going to share. He glanced at her and she gave a slight nod. "In the vein of cooperation, I have someone here with me who has been listening in on the conversation. Her name is Anisa and she found Vaughn on my family's property. He was in bad shape and she nursed him back to health."

After exchanging courtesies, Hudson brought Hawk up to date on the rest.

"Is it possible my cousin is involved in some kind of covert operation?" Hudson needed to clear the air on that first.

"I highly doubt it," Hawk said. "Despite what the movies try to make us all believe, most of us don't join those black-water-type organizations when we're discharged. Most of us are done with that kind of work or we would have stayed in the military in the first place. A couple here and there might go into lucrative private security fields, but Vaughny never mentioned anything of the kind. He wasn't interested. In fact, all he wanted to do was go home and work the land. Said he'd seen enough desert for one lifetime and now he wanted to get back to fields of bluebonnets in spring and working cattle. Said he wanted to get back to a simple life. Believe me when I say working for the government can be frustrating. We follow orders even when we don't agree with a decision or face disciplinary action. Vaughny seemed done to me. If he's doing someone a favor, it seems like word would get around."

"Did he mention anything about making a pitstop before heading home?" Hudson asked.

"Not that I can think of," Hawk said. "My best guess is he went to find Katy, or at the very least see if she was married with kids by now."

"Makes sense he would want closure before coming back to his old life without her," Hudson said. "I'll follow up and check out her social media. Most people post their lives on the internet nowadays. It should be easy enough to track her down and see what she's currently up to."

"You know what she looks like and I have no clue," Hawk pointed out. "You're the best one for the job there."

"I'll dig around and let you know what I find out," Hudson promised.

"This is a good number for me. The line is encrypted, so communication should be safe. How about on your end?" Hawk said.

"I'll send a text from my personal phone, so you'll have that number," Hudson said, doing it right then before he got distracted or ended up down a different rabbit hole and lost track. "There. You should have the new number."

"Got it," Hawk said. "I'll respond right now so you have mine."

"By the way, how did you get this number?" Hudson asked.

"I convinced your security company to patch me in. They refused to give it to me," Hawk explained before ending the call.

Good to know they could be counted on. Hudson's personal cell rang almost immediately. He checked the screen and then stared up at Anisa. "It's my uncle."

"WE'RE ALL HERE and want to help find Vaughn," Hudson's uncle began the conversation. She sat back and listened, amazed at how quickly the family had come together for Vaughn. The whole concept was so foreign to her that she could scarcely imagine having this kind of support. Deep down, this is exactly what she wished for her little bean. To grow up in a world where differences could be set aside when trouble reared its head.

"Who is here?" Hudson asked.

"Kellan, Rafe, Morgan, Nick, Rowan, Tanner, Travis, and Keith. All of your cousins," Keif said. There was a quick round of hellos before the conversation became solemn again.

Anisa couldn't imagine having so many people in her corner. It was a shame the family fought so much and seemed to have divided itself down the middle. At least the sides were coming together on their own accord now with Hudson as the go-between.

"We should probably conference Adam into the call," Hudson said.

"That won't be necessary," his uncle said. "This is family business."

Hudson issued a sharp sigh. He seemed to see the whole family as one unit while his uncle had drawn a line. She could almost feel the tension entering the conversation when it was brought up that both sides should work together. She could only hope they would get past their differences and come together for Vaughn.

"We'll do this your way but understand that I'm involving my side of the family," Hudson stated, unable or unwilling to let that go. "Everyone wants to pitch in and locate Vaughn without wasting valuable time."

"Come on, Dad," one of the male voices on the other side said. "Hudson is right. We need all hands on deck for this one."

A low hum of agreement came through the line. Hudson seemed to realize when to keep quiet and let the majority rule. The tide appeared to be flowing in his direction. From the outside looking in, it was easy to see the family cared deeply about one another even though they were also stubborn as the day was long.

"When is it going to be enough?" One of the others asked. "The Marshall is gone. Uncle Brody has had a stroke. Most of us avoid each other despite living on the same property. Mom is in jail. When are we going to say enough fighting? When are we going to start working together to solve a problem, instead of using everything that happens as an excuse to push us further apart?"

"Kellan and Rafe are both right," Hudson's uncle finally said after a long pause. "Let's involve as many people as we can. The more minds, the better."

"Good," Hudson said and Anisa could hear the relief in his voice. It was like a thousand-pound weight was lifted from his shoulders and some of the tension lines on his forehead eased as he updated the family on everything they knew so far.

"I have Katy's social media page up. There hasn't been a new post in eight months," the voice she recognized as Rafe said.

"Katy goes missing in action eight months ago. Vaughn gets out six months ago. And he's just now showing up on the property?" Hudson's recap drew a chorus of uh-huhs. "Do we know where she was living at the time?"

"I personally lost track of her after she left Lone Star Pass," Kellan said.

"Same here," Hudson agreed. "Is there anything on her page about getting married or having kids?"

"No," Rafe said. "I'm not seeing anything like that. This page looks abandoned."

"Which could mean she moved to another platform," Kellan pointed out.

"Or got too busy with life to keep posting," one of the others said.

"What was her frequency when she used to post?" Hudson asked.

"Not often," Rafe said. "Every few weeks or so. She has the obligatory Bluebonnet pics every spring, but nothing since a Happy New Year post."

"Do you recognize any of the faces in her pictures?" Hudson asked.

"There are none. She mainly posts pictures with just her in them or solely of a landscape," Rafe responded. "There are a couple of food pictures in here."

"Any idea where she was living based on the posts?" Hudson asked.

"Looks like here in Texas, but, no, I can't tell for certain," Rafe said.

"Hudson, where are you?" the voice Anisa recognized as his uncle asked.

"I'm in Texas," was all Hudson said by way of response.

"What do you think about coming here to Lone Star Pass? It might be easier if we're all in the same room," his uncle said.

Hudson frowned.

"As much as I'd like that, I have someone with me who is being targeted by the same people Vaughn is," he said. "Her name is Anisa."

"Well then, if that's the case, I'd rather they be led here, where there are plenty of us to cover for you, keep her safe, and catch the bastards," his uncle said with conviction.

The security guard who was wearing mirrored sunglasses ran to the kitchen door. Paul grabbed the door jamb and popped his head inside.

"We need to get you guys out of here. Someone is coming and it doesn't look good," he said.

Anisa's heart dropped at the expression on his face.

12

"We have to go. We'll call you when we can." Hudson didn't wait for a response from his uncle. He grabbed Anisa's hand and linked their fingers before locking gazes with Paul. "Which way?"

"You guys go out the back and race around to your vehicle. I'll head out the front and head off anyone who comes this way in case there are others," Paul said. "Be on the lookout for an Off-Road vehicle with—"

"Got it," Hudson said, wasting no time heading for the back door as he fished keys out of his pocket. He handed over his cell to Anisa as they made a run for it. At least he'd been able to get a meal inside her before they needed to head back to the ranch. Uncle Keif had been right. The ranch was the safest place for them now that everyone in the family was going to be involved.

The back porch had a locked screen door. The screened-in porch with the flimsy wood frame would be no match for the heel of Hudson's boot.

"Stand back a second," he said, tucking her behind him. He fired off a kick, delivering it straight to the lock. The wood splintered, just as he'd hoped. One more kick and it cracked in half, wood debris flying.

Hudson led the way to the BMW. He hit the key fob before they arrived so opening the passenger door was quick and easy. He had no idea how long it would be before Off-Road got to them or if there were others, so there was no time to waste.

Anisa climbed inside and closed her own door as he bolted toward the driver's seat. The engine hummed with the push of a button. At least they were in a different vehicle now and should be more difficult to track.

"How do you think they found us?" Anisa asked.

"I'm guessing through my cell phone," he stated, unsure how since he'd made a point of turning off all those apps that unwittingly tracked folks and their every move.

"Let's turn it off," she said.

"I might just toss it out the window instead," he said. If someone can hack into it remotely, they can access the information there. I have no idea how to factory reset the thing."

He navigated away from the bed and breakfast, thinking it would have been nice to spend a night there if only to get a chance to reset for Anisa.

"Hold on. I know what to do," he said. "I saw a body of water not too far from here. We can grab the masking tape out of my duffel bag and find a good rock."

If they got to the small lake first and had enough time to complete the mission, it was a perfect idea. If not, they'd be essentially handing themselves over to the jerk intent on getting to Anisa. There was no way Hudson was allowing anything bad to happen to her. Period.

He glanced over and she looked a little pale.

"How are you doing? Are you all right?" he asked.

"Fine. It's all the bumps on this road. Nothing I can't handle and you don't need to slow down," she insisted, looking like she was about to lose her stomach.

"There's probably something in my duffel you could use if you can't hold it in much longer," he stated, glancing in the rearview and seeing Paul follow at a safe distance. Paul's gray truck would block most of the BMW from view from anyone trying to come up from behind. Off-Road could easily get around the truck though. As long as the cell was inside the vehicle with them, Off-Road could track their movements if that was the case.

Hudson bit back a few choice words.

"I'll be fine," Anisa said. "Let's just get rid of that phone."

Hudson rocketed toward the small lake. A bumpy three long minutes later, he pulled off to the side of the road. Anisa jumped out almost immediately and it took a second for her to make it over to the driver's side where he'd initially placed his duffel in the backseat.

He realized it had been a mistake to use his cell once Paul had given him a new one. Old habits were hard to break and he must have subconsciously thought Uncle Keif would at the very least recognize the number and pick up. It was a costly mistake.

Cell phone in hand, he grabbed duct tape from his emergency pack as Anisa located a rock the size of a brick. She handed it over and he taped the cell to the rock. "The lake is small and isn't far from here. It'll be faster if I go on my own."

She nodded, grabbed his forearm, and planted a quick kiss on his cheek. "Be careful," she said.

"Wait in the SUV and lock the doors," he said, feeling a blast in the center of his chest after the kiss. It wasn't much, barely a peck, and yet it struck his heart with the force of a jet.

She started around the back of the vehicle.

"In the driver's seat. Just in case I don't make it back in time," he stated.

She shook her head.

"You'll be back," she said in an overly confident voice. It was the kind of voice people used when they were trying to convince themselves as much as the other person. It didn't convey a whole lot of confidence. He understood why she would feel on shaky ground. He'd become her lifeline in the past twenty-four hours and vice versa. It also struck him how fast two people could get to know each other when lives were on the line.

Hudson raced through the trees, thankful it wouldn't be dark for another hour. He realized he'd left his new cell inside the BMW as he bolted toward the small lake. He made it to the water's edge in a time that would have made his high school track coach proud.

He drew his brick-fisted hand back as far as it would go. Like a coil releasing, he stepped into the throw and watched his cell phone soar half a football field away. That should do the trick, he thought before turning around the way he came a few seconds ago. There was no time to waste as he pushed off tree trunks and struggled to keep balance when the toe of his boot got caught in the underbrush.

The whole episode couldn't have taken more than ten minutes, so he was shocked when he returned to the spot he could have sworn he left Anisa, to find both vehicles gone. He glanced left and then right, trying to get a visual and came up empty. In that moment, it was as though Hudson's entire world caved in. The earth tipped on its axis, and all the air was sucked out of the universe. His heart hammered the inside of his ribcage as white-hot anger boiled through his veins. Panic formed a knot in his gut.

Stressing out wouldn't help matters, he reminded. Keeping a cool head was the reason he was one of the best trackers in the country. This wasn't the time to lose his cool no matter how much his emotions fought to take the wheel.

It also occurred to him Off-Road would be tracking his cell and could show up any second to this very spot. The realization sent him back inside the tree line and circling back toward the bed and breakfast.

Going this way, he would most likely pass Off-Road and could potentially get a description of the guy. The lake had been too far off the road to notice when Anisa and Paul had disappeared. Paul might have assumed Anisa's baby belonged to Hudson and, therefore, prioritized protecting her and the baby first and foremost. A thought like that one, like of Hudson being married with a kid, would normally cause Hudson's throat to close up. This time, an unexplained warmth spread through him. He tucked those thoughts somewhere deep inside.

After running several minutes with branches slapping him in the face, Hudson stopped. Trees in Texas weren't particularly tall but finding a nice one to climb would give him a height advantage plus have the added benefit of making it difficult for Off-Road to see Hudson on the side of the road. Knowing what was coming at him was half the battle.

Hudson located a sturdy tree limb and then climbed until the branches swayed in the wind. Mother Nature picked this moment in time to send gray-swirling clouds across the sky. The air thickened with what felt a whole lot like the threat of rain. Lone Star Pass had sustained a two-year drought and was reaching critical mass. Of course, storms like the one brewing had threatened before. He'd even been outside when a couple droplets of rain spilled out. But the drought was still on and he figured these clouds would peter out too.

At the top of the tree where he could hang onto the trunk, he could see the sun retreating. There was no sign of any vehicles though. Had he misread the situation? Was Off-Road a step ahead of them?

Hudson went back through his thoughts, sifting through them to find his mistake. Paul was trustworthy. He'd been the one to deliver the news someone was coming in an off-road vehicle. Hudson had assumed that meant *the* off-road vehicle from downtown Austin. He'd made the leap instantly when, in fact, there were plenty of off-road vehicles in this area. Mudding was a big sport and even the lack of rain wouldn't matter. These guys would find any lake or water source to drive near, in, or around.

Paul had been the one to sound the alarm about Off-Road. It made sense someone tracking them would use Hudson's cell phone to do it. But how would they have figured out it was him?

The answer came to him almost immediately. His license plate could be traced back to him. It was possible Off-Road had picked up Hudson's license plate and then gotten his name and data. Every time he figured one thing out, two questions pushed to the forefront. How did any of this relate to Katy? Or Vaughn?

Without any means to communicate with his family or Hawk, Hudson was stranded. He trusted Anisa with his life, so something must've happened to spook her or she was being chased. Paul was gone as well. Hudson's mind bounced all over, going to some pretty dark places. If anything happened to Anisa or the baby...

Hudson stopped himself right there. Nothing was going to happen. They were fine. She could be leading Off-Road away from Hudson in order to give him a chance to piece everything together and then hide. She wouldn't leave him stranded.

He could always hike back to the bed and breakfast if there was no activity on the road. He needed to give it a little more time before he jumped to conclusions or set off toward the B&B. Patience was fine when he was tracking poachers. He was beginning to realize how little he had when it came to being worried about Anisa and the baby.

While he sat there, waiting, his mind wandered over to Katy. He remembered her as being a sweet person in high school. What could she have possibly gotten herself involved in that could cause this kind of backlash? Had she asked the favor of Vaughn? If it was true that his cousin still held a torch for her, he would have done anything she asked. Or maybe the request came from someone she knew?

Hudson's mind immediately snapped to Katy possibly getting into a relationship with the wrong person. She might have dated someone she didn't realize was a criminal or someone powerful. This person would have had the kind of pull to disappear right under the noses of Austin PD.

Of course, it was possible they were told to step aside. Who would have that kind of power? Governor, for one. There could be others in politics with enough power to pull a switch like that one. They would have to be high up and influential. This seemed more in line with what might have happened than a secret blackwater-type organization being involved. Hawk had made a good point there. If all Vaughn wanted to do was go back to the ranch and claim his spot, then...

Hold on a second. Speaking of Katy and politics. Wasn't

she the niece of a prominent senator? Politics and people disappearing? It wouldn't be the first time. Hudson needed to have his phone so he could send out a message to the group. Being cut off from everyone and everything made him want to put his fist through something.

The sound of a twig snapping below drew his attention and sent his pulse skyrocketing. He couldn't get a clear visual through the leaves and the person or animal was just out of range to be able to tell by the sound.

Thick clouds covered what little was left of daylight, making it feel like it was ten o'clock at night. Lightning shot across the sky. Hudson scanned the area below. Still, he couldn't make out what was down there. Thunder rolled, drowning out all other sounds. The wind whipped up, causing branches to lash around and the tree trunk he was on to sway. All he could hope at this point was that the tree was strong enough to withstand the winds. Lack of water for the past two years was bringing down trees left and right without much force from winds on the occasion a storm threatened. The damage after the last winter storm blew through looked like a hurricane had struck downtown Lone Star Pass.

This one seemed to be working up to a real fireworks show. Even the winds masked the sounds from below as they picked up speed, taking away his ability to gauge whether or not someone was closing in on him. There was no sign of headlights coming from either direction.

Hudson retrieved his Sig Sauer from his ankle holster and palmed the weapon. He pointed the gun straight down below since it would be easier to adjust his aim than start from scratch with his hand waist high. It was the same reason law enforcement officers walked into a raid with their Glocks leading the way.

Constantly skimming the area, Hudson stayed perfectly still.

A figure came into view. Female. Frantic. He would recognize Anisa anywhere.

But where was the SUV, and where was Paul?

13

Anisa searched the trees for Hudson as panic mounted. She'd already passed the spot where she'd dropped him off. Had Off-Road gotten to him? There'd been no way to tell him what Paul had seen coming. Off-Road had circled around like he was heading them off at the pass. Paul's associate had seen him coming from the opposite direction when they were back at the bed and breakfast.

Or had he circled back to the B&B? Was he still at the lake? Or had he gotten lost on his way back?

He was a tracker, so the last option didn't seem likely. Even though this wasn't his family's ranch, he'd explained what it was like to track poachers and the same skills would apply despite the lack of familiarity with the landscape here. Plus, his ranch was so vast there was no way he could have memorized every inch.

Wind whipped her hair around, the end stinging her cheeks like tiny pinpricks. She pulled strands from the corner of her mouth as she pushed her hair away from her face so she could see clearly. She'd called Hawk from

Hudson's new cell the minute she'd been in the clear according to Paul. He was around here somewhere, searching the woods for Hudson, doubling their efforts.

Hawk had asked for their exact location. Said he'd see what he could do. The conversation wasn't exactly reassuring.

"Anisa," came Hudson's familiar voice, cutting through the wind. She glanced around, unable to see him anywhere she looked. Something stirred in the tree above her. It dawned on her...Hudson was climbing down to her. Relief didn't begin to describe the feeling washing over her at seeing him again. Fear had gripped her when she didn't see him after circling back. Several scenarios ran on repeat in her mind, none of them good. Tears pricked the backs of her eyes as he climbed down. It was too soon to relax but his presence had a calming effect on her like no other.

She stood her ground and surveyed the area, ensuring it would be safe once he got his boots on the ground again. He immediately brought her into an embrace and whispered, "I was afraid I'd lost you."

The words were heavy with fear and regret. Lightning streaked across the sky, illuminating thick gray clouds that were moving at a fast clip. The only thing that mattered was they were together again.

"We better get out of here before the storm hits," Anisa said, thinking there was a whole other squall brewing behind Hudson's dark roast eyes. Her chest squeezed as she looked up at him, thinking no one had ever spoken to her in a tone that caused such a reaction in her body. He blinked a couple of times and she couldn't help but think some people would kill to have those long, thick lashes. She could get lost in those eyes.

"From now on, we stick together. No matter what," he

said, then clenched his jaw muscle like he was holding back emotions that seemed difficult to keep at bay.

Rather than voice a response when words felt inadequate, Anisa pushed up to her tiptoes and kissed him. Their last kiss was still imprinted in her thoughts and she needed to see if her reaction was a fluke or force of nature. The second those thick lips of his pressed down on hers, she knew. Her reaction wasn't a one-time affair. The swirling sensation low in her belly had never been so strong. But then, she'd never been with a man this perfect.

"Keep that in mind," he said after pulling back. He caught her gaze and held it for a few seconds, long enough for her to see they were both as affected by those kisses. He reached for her hand with his left before linking their fingers. In his right hand, she noticed a gun. It was the one she'd seen him carry before and a reminder of the danger they were presently in. There was no time to talk about the feelings welling up inside her at the thought of losing him.

"We're this way," she said, motioning back toward the way she came. Anisa was always calm in the moment, her nurse's training kicked in and she went into autopilot. She had a strange and uncanny ability to shelve her emotions until a time when she could deal with them. The onslaught came later, and this would rate right up there with an avalanche when this was all said and done.

A thought struck as they navigated back toward the SUV. Did she ever take time to process her emotions? Or were they all bottlenecked inside her, struggling for just the right timing to release? Just the thought of T.J. made her tear up and her mind go into lockdown mode. In fact, she couldn't remember the last time she let herself have a good cry.

Instead of taking time to process, had she just kept

herself so busy she dropped into bed every night? Don't even get her started on her issues with her mother. The woman paid just enough attention to Anisa to keep the neighbors from calling CPS. The one time her mother had slipped when Anisa was in grade school, the teacher had made the call. An investigator came by and, with an overworked caseload, made it easy for Anisa to convince him that everything really was fine. Anisa had plastered a smile on that day too. Just like so many other days. And now? She was bone-tired from all the fake smiles. Her jaws hurt. But she would keep going because that was what she knew how to do.

She would push through this situation and then go back to her life. She would push through the pain of leaving Hudson behind; he had become her lifeline. She would push through the loneliness by throwing herself into getting ready for the baby.

It was time to unpack all the boxes at her apartment and put the drama and loss that came with Kevin behind her, along with all the other baggage she'd picked up along the way in life. Why was it so easy to pack the bags and so hard to unpack them? Hers were stuffed full and she had yet to hit her thirtieth birthday. She wasn't sure what that said about her, but she was determined not to let the past define her future—a future she was starting to think could be possible with Hudson.

Anisa shut those thoughts down right then and there. Hudson had said he missed her. He'd said he was frantic with worry about her. Of course, she was pregnant and almost everyone she'd encountered after the bump started showing had gone out of their way to be kind. More doors had been opened for her than she could count. Even young folks got in on the act. The part that wasn't so awesome was all the strangers who wanted to touch her bump when she finally started showing. Those she could do without even though she appreciated their intentions.

Trees slapped her in the face as she felt the first droplets of rain sting her face.

"Do you feel that?" Hudson asked, and she could scarcely hear him over the howling winds.

"Rain? Yes," she admitted, thinking it had been far too long since they'd had a good soaking. They'd had nothing more than sprinkles here and there and the ground showed it. The clay soil cracked, creating deep caverns, and in some cases threatening to swallow cars whole. The land was parched as far as the eye could see on a good day.

The raindrops dried up almost as fast as they'd arrived. The threat, however, still hung in the air, making breathing hard and reminding them Mother Nature could unleash her force at any second and on any whim. The heavy air weighed down her lungs as she practically gasped for air. She wished she could ask for a break or for Hudson to slow the pace at the very least, but Off-Road was out here somewhere. They had no real idea where, only that he was closing in.

Anisa led them back to the SUV, which was parked in the tree line off the main road. She immediately bolted to the passenger side. Hudson glanced at the spot where a bullet grazed the rear side of the vehicle. The right brake light was out.

Once inside, he immediately started the vehicle and heard click-click-click.

Hudson released a string of curses that would make a sailor proud as he tried to start the vehicle one more time.

"They found it," Anisa said. "They've been here."

"Someone most likely messed with the battery cable," he said. "Let me check it out."

He popped the hood as she grabbed the cell phone and got Hawk on the line.

"I found him, but someone has tampered with our vehicle," she said, wondering where Paul could be.

"Okay, good job," Hawk confirmed. "Where is Hudson now?"

"Checking the battery wires," she said.

"I have friends on the way," Hawk stated in a voice that said he approved.

She figured they were the kinds of 'friends' who knew how to get out of a jam like this and had probably seen a whole lot worse during their time in the service.

"It'll take a minute for them to arrive, so keep me posted on your location at all times," he said. "That's important, okay?"

"Got it," she stated, thinking this was all so surreal. Granted, she respected all the men who fought for their country more than words could express. The sacrifices they and their families made were unimaginable to her. It kept her problems in perspective too. She hadn't faced an unknown enemy, put her own child to bed hungry, or anything of the sort. She'd drawn the short straw when it came to parents and was painfully aware of the fact. But she couldn't feel a bit sorry for herself when men and women were out there giving their lives willingly so that others could be free. It was a grounding thought.

"How is he doing?" Hawk asked.

"He's heading back inside now," she stated.

Hudson reclaimed the driver's seat and pushed the button. No keys for this vehicle. The engine hummed to life.

"He got it to start," she said.

"All right. Now we're in business," Hawk said and there was a twinge of excitement in his voice.

"Who is on the phone?" Hudson asked as he put the gearshift in reverse.

"Hawk," she stated.

Hudson gave an approving nod. "Tell him I lost my security detail."

She relayed the message.

"That doesn't sound good," Hawk stated. "Although, the man might be doing his job drawing the threat away from the two of you."

"Let's hope so," she said before relaying the message to Hudson.

"We need to get ahold of Paul," Hudson said to her.

"I need to hang up now," Anisa said to Hawk.

"Which way are you headed?" he asked.

She glanced at the compass on the screen of the BMW. "Northwest."

"Got it. Text if you change course. Okay?" he asked, and she figured the question was just making sure his request registered. His clipped military tone said he was used to giving orders, being in the driver's seat. With the help he was offering, she didn't mind.

"Will do," she said before ending the call. She turned to Hudson as headlights came up from behind. "I don't have Paul's number. Hawk is the only contact in this phone other you're your brothers and we tossed yours."

The headlights flashed.

"DOESN'T LOOK like we need Paul's phone number after all," Hudson said to Anisa. "He's right behind us."

"How can you tell?" she asked.

"Off-Road's headlights were higher. The ones behind us belong to a truck," he said. "Since they're flashing, I'm assuming Paul is trying to give us the signal it's him."

Hudson slowed the BMW enough to allow the truck to pull up beside them. Paul's window was down as he drove up on the right. Anisa hit the button and her window came down. For the time they were apart, Hudson had been losing his mind. Anisa was important to him and when the danger was in the rearview, he intended to tell her. He could only hope that by then he would have figured out what he was offering. He'd even grown attached to the baby growing inside her ever since feeling the little one move.

"Phone," Paul shouted with a shrug.

Hudson nodded. There hadn't been time to organize and, besides, they thought they were all sticking together. Life had another plan.

"Slow down," Paul said.

Hudson slowed to a stop, surveying the mirrors to make sure no one could sneak up on them.

"There's more than one," Paul said.

"Off-road vehicles?" Hudson asked.

Paul nodded.

"I wonder if that's how Off-Road escaped the law earlier," Anisa said.

"It's possible," Hudson agreed. If there were several it could explain the confusion with law enforcement. He still had a difficult time figuring out how Austin PD had lost Off-Road in the first place, even if there was more than one. Had the chopper confused the issue? Was that the problem?

Lighting shot across the sky like a bullet. Thunder boomed so hard it shook the ground. The storm wasn't nearly finished with them. All he could say was Mother

Nature needed to bring it on instead of these empty threats. The sky was nothing but hues of black and dark gray, not a star to be found. Under normal circumstances, the clouds indicated the level of storm coming. Dark, rolling gray clouds like these would normally warn of a downpour. With the fits and starts they'd had in the past two years with no precipitation to speak of, he'd reserve his opinion until nature proved itself. It wouldn't do any good to get his hopes up.

"What's the quickest way out of here?" Hudson asked. "The one with the most options? I need to get her to the ranch."

Paul spoke into an earpiece.

"Follow me," he said after a few seconds passed. "We're bringing in another team. I believe you know Hawk. Between the two of us, we'll get you home safe."

"Go for it," Hudson said.

Paul nodded before pulling into the lead. A vehicle came from behind, effectively sandwiching them in a protective mode. Despite the added security, Hudson sat on pins and needles for the entire ride to the ranch.

"Wow," Anisa muttered as they pulled onto the lane to the main house. "Even at night, this place is impressive."

He turned onto the drive and was immediately waved through the guard shack.

"Thank you," was all he could say in response. Hudson was so used to Firebrand Ranch that he hadn't looked at it from an outsider's perspective in a long time. He and his family couldn't exactly be objective, having grown up here.

"*This* is your family legacy?" she asked with a whole lot of admiration.

"It is," he stated and his chest filled with pride. He was

looking at the place from a new lens tonight, seeing from her fresh perspective. Firebrand Ranch was home.

"Well, I can see why you would have a hard time walking away from all this," she said, the awe in her tone reminded him how fortunate he'd been living here his entire life. It was strange too because he thought he was good at being grateful. Guess he still had a lot to learn and a ways to go.

"The land is the best part," he said after a thoughtful pause. Then he saw something that warmed his heart. "Or at least it was until now."

Lining the drive as he neared the main house were his brothers and cousins. All were present, save for Vaughn. There was a space in between Tanner and Travis that was clearly meant for their sibling, a hole Hudson intended to have filled as soon as humanly possible.

Anisa reached over and touched his arm. A light touch shouldn't feel so personal, so intimate in the way that it did.

Hudson pulled and parked. By some force of magic, a.k.a. his family, his truck was already home waiting for him.

"That's amazing," Anisa said, seeming to realize what they'd done at almost exactly the same time as he did.

Funny how it sometimes took a traumatic event or loss for a family to really pull together. There'd been plenty of those on the ranch since the Marshall's death, but they'd only served to drive a deeper wedge. It was interesting to note how the one man who'd kept the family at odds all these years ended up being the one who unwittingly set off a chain of events that pulled them back together.

Hudson exited the BMW and quickly moved around to the passenger side. "How tired are you?"

"Beyond exhausted," she admitted.

"I can have everyone meet up at my house rather than here," he said.

"Don't do that," she protested. "I don't want to be any trouble. And, honestly, I could probably lay my head down anywhere at this point and be fine."

Something deep within him that he couldn't quite explain wanted, no needed, her to be comfortable. And yet he knew she would never ask for that for herself.

"It might be better for the baby if you get a good night of sleep," he pointed out.

She stood there for a moment as the others made their way over in small clumps.

"Good point," she finally relented, letting better judgment rule. "Okay, but just drop me off and then you can come back and work."

"No one will mind if I stay home, Anisa. You and the baby are important to me. I need you both healthy," he said, wondering when he'd become such a softy. It was her and there was something about her pregnancy that brought out all his protective instincts. Maybe it was the fact the two of them were all alone in the world and he'd felt the same for so long despite being surrounded by people. "Besides, the others can come to me. There's no reason we can't meet up at the cabin."

He finally understood how his brothers had met their person and immediately knew. A lightning bolt had struck him out of the blue and he realized Anisa was the one for him. It was starting to make sense they didn't wait for some magic date or amount of information about the other person that made them decide to get married. When lightning struck, a person knew.

Did Anisa feel the same way?

The chemistry between them was electric. She had to feel it too. Right? He'd seen it in her eyes. Would she risk her heart again after she'd been burned in the worst possible way? Being cheated on said so much more about her partner than it did about her. And yet, she'd made it clear she blamed herself for going down that road again with her ex. Could she allow herself to trust again? To trust him?

He hoped she could because he'd never felt this way about anyone else and, when the time was right, he had every intention of telling her what she'd come to mean to him. He would put it all on the line and let her decide once she had all the facts.

After a round of introductions and hugs, Hudson let the family know the plan.

"Why don't you stay with her? We can split up and have some people working at the main house, while a few go back with you. This will allow us to keep in touch," Adam said, holding up his cell phone.

"I agree," Kellan said in a move that pretty much shocked everyone standing there. Hudson couldn't remember a time those two agreed on anything.

Thunder rumbled in the distance. Clouds rolled. Rain threatened. And yet for the first time in a long time, Hudson believed everything was going to work out at home. *Home?* Funny, because when he thought of home now, Anisa and the baby came to mind.

"Sounds like a plan," Hudson said. It warmed his heart that everyone accepted Anisa with open arms.

He held open the passenger door for her. She climbed back inside. She'd ducked her head, chin to chest, and he realized she was trying to hide her face. She was a very private person and wouldn't want anyone to know if her emotions were getting the best of her.

"Brax, Fallon, and the twins will meet you at home," Adam said after a quick pow-wow with Kellan and the others. "We'll have a quick meeting here before they head over so we know who will be working on what."

Hudson nodded, appreciating the mix of brothers and cousins who were assigned to stay with him and Anisa. No more lines drawn in the sand. No more split between the family. The way it should have always been.

"You have one amazing family," Anisa said, dropping her hands to cradle her baby. He wondered if she even realized she did it or if it was the workings of her subconscious. Either way, she was going to be an incredible mother, and he hoped he'd be able to stick around in her life to see it.

Anisa was quiet on the way to his house. His mind had shifted gears, and was already trying to work out the next steps to figure out where Vaughn could be. He hoped his cousin was somewhere safe, protecting Katy until the threat could be neutralized.

He needed to update Hawk on what was happening. The man had to be at least partially responsible for their safe ride to the ranch. And then there was Anisa's immediate needs.

"Are you hungry?" he asked as he parked the vehicle.

"I could eat those meatballs pretty much anytime, anyplace. No need to be hungry for those," she said with a small smile before immediately biting back a yawn.

"Meatballs it is," he said. "Then, we get you to bed."

He exited the vehicle before circling around the front to open her door. They had probably a half hour of privacy before the others descended on the place. He reached for her hand and then linked their fingers.

The minute they walked inside the house, Hudson felt the hairs on the back of his neck prick. He flipped on the light and scanned the open-concept room. Nothing immediately drew his eye.

"Do you feel that?" he asked Anisa, thinking his radar might be pulling overtime after everything they'd been through.

"Yes," she said as she tightened her grip on his hand.

And then Hudson glanced down. In front of him, big red splotches dotted the wood floors. Blood.

14

"Whoever is here or came through is obviously hurt." Anisa realized she was stating the obvious. "My mind immediately snapped to Vaughn."

"Makes perfect sense. He called me to help. If he's in trouble and wants to stay under the radar, he would likely show up here," Hudson said. He bent down and retrieved his gun, then shut off the light. "Just in case."

His next move was protective. He tucked her behind him as they moved through the space, arm against the wall. The fact Hudson kept her with him said he'd learned his lesson from their earlier plan with the cell phone. He didn't seem ready to make that mistake again and neither was she. Those minutes—hour?—she was away from Hudson were the absolute worst. She'd lost loved ones before and was all-too-familiar with the feeling, the emptiness. This was so much worse. The other losses had cut a hole in her heart.

This had taken a piece of her soul.

She'd had the overwhelming feeling she'd be half a

person without Hudson, which was odd because she'd never been one of those people who felt incomplete without a boyfriend or spouse. Unloved? That was a different story. But she'd always been whole.

Anisa couldn't see a thing except in the moments when lightning struck. The low near-constant rumble of thunder shook the walls. If Vaughn was here, wouldn't he call out to his cousin?

Icy fingers gripped her spine at the thought it could be someone else. Someone who wanted her dead for reasons she still couldn't fully comprehend. Being seen with Vaughn was her crime. Whoever was after him wanted her too. Again, she was trying to process a world where this could happen. She'd believed her job was the most excitement in her life. It kept her hopping to be sure. For months, the pregnancy had taken center stage.

Funny how being in a life or death situation had her reevaluating her priorities, seeing things clearly for maybe the first time in a very long time. She hadn't been certain she could handle being a single mother until now. She could do this. Because the only worse than losing Hudson would be losing the baby. Anisa had grown attached to the little bean without realizing how deep the bond had become. Until now, she thought the baby might be better off if she changed her mind and gave it up for adoption.

Now? She realized she was capable of doing anything she set her mind to. She had put herself through nursing school despite a lack of funds and support. She'd worked two jobs to cover her expenses and be able to pay for classes. She'd gotten up at four o'clock in the morning despite not at all being a morning person. She'd bought her own car.

What she finally realized was that she didn't need a

family member to make her feel validated. Anyone would be proud of her accomplishments but the one who mattered most was her. She was proud of herself. And from now on, her opinion would be the one that mattered above all else.

She took a step forward as Hudson stopped. She ran smack into his back but he didn't so much as make a peep. Thunder covered any noise she was making. Hudson, however, couldn't be heard at all. She chalked it up to his tracking skills and reasoned it was why he was so good at it.

A few of his family members would be arriving soon. Would they show in time if this wasn't Vaughn? Even if they called right now it would take them close to half an hour to arrive. Who else could possibly be here if not Hudson's cousin? Another problem was that Vaughn was already injured. Was he bleeding out somewhere inside his cousin's home?

And then she heard the sound that stopped her in her tracks. The door opened in the hall closet and a large man stepped out. The glint of metal said he was ready to shoot.

Anisa tugged at Hudson's shoulder, trying to pull him back and out of the hallway before the shooter could fire. He took a bigger step backward than she anticipated and caught the toe of her shoe with his heel. He stumbled back, nearly falling over in the process. Anisa tripped, fell, and landed on her backside. The back of her head smacked against the wall.

"Hudson?"

She recognized Vaughn's voice immediately as a light flipped on in the hallway. He made a move toward them and sat down instead, leaning against the wall.

"Are you okay?" Hudson asked her, fear in his voice.

"Yes. Go to him." She practically shooed him away. She

wasn't woozy or seeing stars. She just needed a minute to collect herself.

The front door opened. Were the others here? The fact no one called out sent a cold chill racing down her spine.

Hudson glanced from her to Vaughn. She motioned for him to worry about his cousin as she pushed up to standing. As he practically carried his cousin into the bedroom, she grabbed the gun in Vaughn's hand and turned it toward the mouth of the hallway.

A figure stepped in. A woman. She had a frantic look.

"My name is Katy. Please put that thing away," she said. "I can't explain but we have to get out of here. *Now.*"

"Vaughn is weak and there's no way he can be moved much farther than the bedroom. What is going on?" Anisa demanded.

"My uncle signed a bill that caused a prominent family with connections to lose out on a land deal that would give them rights to develop a piece of property that had been designated as a nature preserve," Katy said. "They threatened to take away everything my uncle loved, so they came for me first. I'm like a daughter to him. He's been hiding me for the past eight months and when they upped their game, he contacted Vaughn's supervisor and found out he was leaving the military. My uncle begged Vaughn to help keep me out of sight until his special officers could track the Raker brothers down. They are the ones behind this."

"Why not arrest the family?" Anisa asked.

"My uncle has proof they're the ones behind this but he said that this family helped him get elected. He's done favors for the family and they were holding it over his head," she admitted, glancing around.

"We have to get Vaughn to the ER," Anisa said. "We need to call an ambulance right now. He doesn't look good and he's losing too much blood. He'll die if he doesn't get the help he needs."

Katy looked like she was blinking back tears. She was short and thin, the complete opposite of Vaughn. She had a delicate nature and seemed as though she'd been pampered her whole life. She also didn't come across like she had a mean bone in her body. Her wide brown eyes and quivering chin revealed how worried she was and how much she cared for Vaughn.

"He got hurt protecting me," she said. "This is my fault. I never should have allowed my uncle to involve him. I just panicked and agreed to whatever he said. But this has to stop now. If Vaughn can't keep me safe, no one can."

"We can figure out all that later. Right now, I need to know if you locked the door behind you," Anisa said, using her stern nursing voice to calm Katy down. The woman looked like she was about to crumble into hysterics and that wouldn't be good for Vaughn or the situation.

"Um, no," Katy said. "I don't think I locked it. I heard a noise when you guys came and panicked. I ran out the back-door so I could go for help if it turned out to be the Rakers."

Anisa highly doubted they would pull right up in a truck and announce their presence but Katy's eyes were wide and her breathing shallow. She was winding up to a full-scale panic attack.

"I'll go lock it. Hudson carried Vaughn into the master bedroom. You can go check on them and see if they need anything," Anisa said. More than anything, she figured Katy needed something to do. She also needed to see that Vaughn was okay at the moment.

She wished she had her cell phone.

"Tell Hudson to call 911 and request an ambulance. I'll be right in after I make sure the door is locked." If the

Rakers were in the area, she hoped the cavalry would be here before they could make it inside the home.

The frightened woman scurried past. Anisa, in turn, made a beeline for the front door now that Katy had an assignment. As she reached for the door, it opened. A man wearing all black with a hoodie and sunglasses covering much of his features snatched her. She tried to scream but the sound of thunder overhead drowned her out.

In two seconds, she was yanked out the door and being dragged toward the trees.

"Hudson!" was all she managed to scream before a hand came over her mouth.

HUDSON COULD HAVE SWORN he heard his name being screamed from somewhere outside. He was tending to his cousin but could have sworn he heard Anisa come into the room behind him. He glanced around in time to see Katy standing there, looking like she was in shock.

"Come over here and hold this on his shoulder," he calmly said to Katy. "Keep pressure on it."

She nodded and complied but for a half-second he was concerned she would just stand there, too stunned to speak. The minute she replaced his hand, he asked, "Where is Anisa?"

"She said to call 911 and request an ambulance. Then, she went to lock the front door," Katy said, her voice robotic but at least she was following directions. His heart went out to her as he could only imagine the ordeal she'd been through.

Hudson made the call as he bolted to the window. He saw Anisa being dragged toward the trees as she fought back. There was one man that he could see and possibly more that he couldn't.

He texted his family to come ASAP as he ran to the front door and then toward the trees. By the time he reached the porch, Anisa had disappeared.

The skies were almost black now. The clouds rolling like a person in a fitful sleep. Lightning struck and thunder boomed as a few raindrops splattered on his forehead. Catching up to the male figure who was almost dragging Anisa through the woods was the easy part. Hudson moved ahead in the direct path and climbed a tree.

The man had kept checking behind. This would give Hudson an advantage. This would give him the element of surprise. He heard a second voice ahead of them. He couldn't allow guy one to take Anisa to the other person who was waiting.

As the man neared, a bolt of lightning provided enough illumination to see him clearly. He wore all black and a hoodie. Hudson waited. Timing was everything. Timing was the difference between Anisa being hurt and them being caught. He had no idea what the second guy had in terms of weapons. He doubted there was anyone else around, so there was that.

Hoodie answered as he walked just below Hudson. He dropped from the tree and landed with one arm around Hoodie's neck and a hand over his mouth.

The guy grunted and tried to elbow Hudson. Anisa gasped but quickly recovered. She immediately started pounding on the guy wearing the hoodie. She drew her knee up and landed a blow where no man wanted a knee.

Hudson had to agree the two of them made one helluva team. When Hoodie dropped to his knees, Hudson continued pressure on his neck until he passed out.

"He won't be out nearly long enough. Sit on him until I get back," he whispered.

She nodded but before she let him go, she kissed him. Then, she sat on Hoodie's back, pinning him to the ground.

Hudson took out the second guy almost as easily. Separate and without weapons, they were no match for a skilled tracker like him. The second guy choked out in less time than the first. Hudson picked the guy up and threw him over his shoulder fireman style. He brought the two together, took off his belt, and tied off the second guy's wrists behind his back.

Then, he sat on top of Hoodie before making a call to Adam to explain the situation. His brother said help was almost there.

Hudson looked at Anisa. Really looked at her. Hands down, she was the strongest woman he'd ever met. He loved that about her.

"I promised myself that I would talk to you when this was all over," he said to her as the sky lit up in a cacophony of lightning.

A few more drops fell as Anisa released tears it seemed like she'd been holding in her entire life. They streamed down her face, mingling with the rain.

"What did you want to say to me?" she asked, bracing herself for disappointment.

"I know people have let you down in the past, Anisa. I'm here to tell you that I will never turn my back on you, cheat on you, or do anything on purpose that could hurt you," he said. "This might sound strange, but I know my mind and I know when I've met someone special. At least, I do now. I've never met anyone like you. I've fallen hard for you," he said, unsure if his sentiment would be welcomed or would push her away. "I love you and I want to spend the rest of my life proving that you can count on me."

Anisa sat there for a long moment like she was taking it all in. The rain started coming down in a steady beat and voices could be heard in the background, coming toward them.

Hudson shouted out to give his brothers and cousins their location.

"I need you in my life," he said. "But I understand if this is all too fast for you. Just understand that I'm willing to wait. Just let me be in your and the baby's lives."

She cradled her bump and smiled.

"I don't think it sounds strange, Hudson. I've never felt this way about another man in my life. You're honorable. You're genuine. You're beautiful," she said.

He couldn't help but chuckle at the last compliment.

"You are," she insisted.

"I don't care what you call me as long as you agree to marry me," he admitted. "I can't exactly get down on one knee right now, but I will. I'll get down on one knee a thousand times until you're ready to say yes."

"I'm ready, Hudson," she said with more of those tears streaming down her face. She was the one who was beautiful. "I love you and I want to be your wife."

Hudson couldn't wait to hold his future wife, his family. And he wasn't the least bit scared. He'd found the one person he wanted to do life with, and he never planned to let her go.

"Where are you?" Morgan shouted. The twins were running, sounding like the equivalent of a stampede.

"Over here," Hudson responded.

"You okay?" Nick asked in between heaves.

"All good here. You made it just in time," Hudson said as his cousins cleared the trees and came into view.

The cavalry had arrived.

"What in tarnation are the Raker brothers doing here?" Nick asked.

"Let's just say the threat is over. Vaughn is safe," Hudson stated. "Katy is free to go home."

15

"This meeting has been a long time coming," Uncle Keif began as the family gathered in the kitchen of the main house. The only person missing was Vaughn, who was still on the downlow with Katy, healing, and waiting until the case against the Rakers came to trial.

Two weeks had passed since the Raker brothers were arrested. Fourteen days into Hudson's engagement, he was still all-in with Anisa. The love of his life stood next to him and he couldn't be prouder she'd accepted his proposal that night in the trees. She had agreed to live on the ranch and, since there'd been a baby boom along with the fact she was expecting, she had taken the position of head nurse. The fact the position had been created just for her didn't matter. There were incidents on the ranch that required medical assistance. She volunteered to step into the role with her whole heart and a smile. Kevin's parents had agreed to move into a casita on the ranch so they could be near their grandchild. As far as Hudson was concerned, the more family around his son or daughter, the better.

Everyone was gathered around the granite island or

sitting at the kitchen table that was suited for a baker's dozen.

"My brother and I have come to a decision," Uncle Keif looked toward Hudson's father. "Brody, do you want to tell the kids and grandkids what we've decided?"

Hudson's father smiled and nodded. He'd been taking it easy as far as duties on the ranch went and thanks to Lucia Firebrand's care. Hudson had never seen his parents happier and he, for one, was glad to see it. His mother deserved the world but seemed content with a house full of family.

"Keifer and I have decided to split everything down the middle and hand over the reins of the ranch to all eighteen of our sons," Hudson's father stated. "Every one of you will have equal share of mineral rights, cattle, and land. My brother and I only want to retain rights to our own houses."

There was a hum of excitement and questions.

"What will your roles be?" Adam asked.

"Mind if I take this one?" Uncle Keif asked Hudson's father.

"Be my guest," his father said.

"Here's the reality. We've messed everything up royally. The two of us have spent a lifetime bickering and picking at each other. We've compared ourselves to each other and competed mercilessly," Uncle Keif explained. "And here's the deal. We have come to the realization that we don't know squat." He put his hand up when there were grumblings. "I'm not talking about the business. We've done okay there and plan to give you fellas and ladies more advice than you probably ever wanted. Somehow, though, you guys have grown up strong in spite of our constant fighting. You are incredible sons and we couldn't be prouder of each one of you. We have faith in you and know that you can do better than we ever did."

Hudson's father was nodding his agreement.

"The sneaky part of this is that it will force you all to work together in a way that we never could. It's our hope that you will renew bonds and work together for the good of the family's future. The ranch will live on prosperously or die in each of your hands and how well you collectively work together," his father said. "Because here's the thing. We are wealthy men with more than enough money in our bank accounts to live out our lives well financially. But we've been completely bankrupt in every other aspect of our relationships. We can do better. We want to do better. And we only hope that you can forgive two old men who want to be better."

Hudson glanced around and there wasn't a dry eye in the room, which made him feel a whole lot better about the tears rolling down his cheeks.

"First of all, I want to thank you both on behalf of me and my brothers," Adam said. "It takes a lot of courage to own up to mistakes and admit them to the people who look up to you and you love even when they may not believe you're doing the right things."

Heads nodded as faces suddenly turned away to face a wall or window, no doubt trying to hide the emotions overflowing.

"Prudence and I have been talking and we don't feel right keeping the main house to ourselves," Adam continued. "We believe this place belongs to everyone and should be shared equally. We hope that holidays can be spent here together with all of the family getting along, if everyone agrees."

More grunts of agreement filled the room.

To Hudson's thinking, there was only one person missing, one seat unfilled at the table and it belonged to Vaughn. He'd dropped off the grid and no one knew his whereabouts, much to everyone's stress.

"The expansion to my home is almost complete, and myself, Prudence, and the baby will be moving in before Thanksgiving," Adam continued. "It has been our hope that everyone can be together at the main house for the holiday."

The smile on Lucia Firebrand's face meant everything to Hudson and he knew the others felt the same way.

"There's a lot of work to be done in order to patch up the different sides of the family," Uncle Keif added.

More heads nodded.

Desire was half the battle, Hudson thought. With everyone on the same page, wanting the same thing, they would figure it out in no time.

"We are better together," Kellan said. "As a unit, working together for the future of the ranch. Now that this legacy is in all of our hands, we have something worth working toward together."

"We have made a lot of mistakes," Hudson's father said. "It's our hope that you can use them to learn from and bring the family closer together rather than an excuse to keep tearing it apart. The future of this family, this business, this ranch is up to the people in this room."

"And all we can ask is for forgiveness," Uncle Keif added. "We're learning from our sons how to support one another instead of tear each other down, and we both want to be part of our grandchildren's lives. Many mistakes have been made but we hope we'll be given a chance to prove our dedication to the family and to helping you all in any way we can."

"Our mistakes are long and hurtful," his father continued.

"Look at how greed has literally ruined my family and cost me a wife," Uncle Keif said. "She never should have gone to the lengths she did, but I'm not willing to let myself off the hook. I never should have let her go down that path or stoked that flame. My wife being in jail is just as much my fault for letting my jealousy get out of control as it is anyone's. I hope I can learn from the mistakes I've made and find a way to prove that I'm not that person anymore. I know it will take time, but I'm willing to put in the work and I'm hoping someday each person in this room will be able to forgive me. I plan to dedicate myself to the family from now on. With Brody's stroke, along with everything else that has happened, I realize how short time can truly be and that tomorrow isn't guaranteed. I've witnessed the consequences that happen when greed and jealousy go unchecked, and I'm embarrassed about the example I've been to my sons and nephews."

His father brought Uncle Keif into a hug.

"I believe that underneath the layers of miscommunication and jealousy in this family," Kellan started, "there is also a whole lot of love there."

All eyes shot to Kellan and Adam, who have had the longest running dislike for each other. Both being the oldest and could be incredibly stubborn.

Adam walked over to Kellan and offered a handshake. Kellan stared at the extended hand for a long moment before slapping it away and bringing Adam into a bear hug. And then Kellan shocked them all by walking straight over to Corbin and embracing his cousin.

"Surely there's divide so big we can't build a bridge," Kellan said to Corbin.

"I'd like to be one family again," Corbin said, emotion swimming in both of their eyes. Acceptance. Healing. Love.

Hudson stepped forward.

"I'd like to make a proposition," he said. "Because in my estimation, we've left someone very important out of the equation. There is someone who is just as important to the success of this ranch as all of us are. Someone who has done nothing but devote his life to the land and the family. Someone who deserves to be included in the family and ranch business plus would serve as a tie-breaker should the family ever take sides. This person has devoted his entire life to making Firebrand Ranch the success it is today. He is one of the first people each of us call when we needed a hand and cared as much about the ranch as anyone in the room. I'd like to nominate Bronc Harris to be a full-fledged member of the family, equal partner, and someone who has an equal vote."

"Does everyone agree?" Uncle Keif asked.

Heads nodded.

"We need to get him in the room," Adam said proudly.

Someone, Hudson wasn't sure who, invited Bronc into the main house kitchen.

He was uncomfortable being inside, being most comfortable in the barn or the bunkhouse. As far as Hudson was concerned, Bronc could stay anywhere he wanted.

He was a man of few words, but his expression said it all when they delivered the news. Chin to chest, he coughed to cover up his emotions. When he brought his head up, his smile was practically ear-to-ear.

"I won't take this responsibility lightly," he promised.

"I think everyone would agree that you are the last person who would take advantage of being an equal partner and that you are the first person who deserves the honor. In all of our eyes, you are family and deserve everything that goes along with it. Good and bad," Hudson stated.

He chuckled and pressed his hand flat against his chest over his heart.

"All I can say at that point is trust me when I say there is far more good in this family than bad," he said.

The room erupted in laughter and congratulations. An excitement and sense of possibility for the future filled the air. And then Hudson walked past the empty chair where his cousin should be.

While the celebration continued, Sheriff Lawler entered the room.

"I'm sorry to break up a celebration with bad news," he said. "The vehicle Vaughn was last believed to be driving was in an accident in Colorado. The vehicle went over the side of the mountain where there was no guardrail and, although no body was found, there was no way Vaughn could have survived the crash. Search teams are continuing to look for Vaughn, but there is a ravine and a river at the bottom of the mountain that could have carried his body away."

Silence swept the room as the sound of rain pinged on the roof. A downpour followed. Rain. There was finally rain.

Shock and disbelief filled the space where there had been laughter and congratulations.

"I'm sorry to break into your evening with such bad news but I wanted to stop by personally and tell you," he said.

Tears stained everyone's faces. There was a whole lot of disbelief that Vaughn could be gone.

"Are you sure?" Uncle Keif finally asked.

"The vehicle went over the side two days ago at dusk. A couple had seen his vehicle at the base of the mountain going up as they were coming down from a hike," Lawler said.

And then a text rolled in on Hudson's phone.

"It's from Vaughn and he's saying that he has something to finish and will be back home as soon as he can," Hudson stated.

The question was...did the text come in before the crash or after?

IF YOU ENJOYED THE FIREBRANDS, I think you'll love my McGannon boys and their canine companions.

Cowboy Reckoning - Intent on proving her brother was murdered a decade ago, Ensley Cartier returns to the one place she vowed to never set foot in again. With the whole town against her, she finds an ally in Levi McGannon. He loves the land and the ranching way of life, but they quickly discover Cattle Cove isn't the innocent town he once believed and somebody wants Ensley buried along with their secrets.

Click here to keep reading a Barb Han book.

ALSO BY BARB HAN

For more of Barb's books, visit www.BarbHan.com.

ABOUT THE AUTHOR

Barb Han is a USA TODAY and Publisher's Weekly Bestselling Author. Reviewers have called her books "heartfelt" and "exciting."

Barb lives in Texas—her true north—with her adventurous family, a poodle mix and a spunky rescue who is often referred to as a hot mess. She is the proud owner of too many books (if there is such a thing). When not writing, she can be found exploring Manhattan, on a mountain either hiking or skiing depending on the season, or swimming in her own backyard.

Sign up for Barb's newsletter at www.BarbHan.com.

Printed in Great Britain
by Amazon